Sons of
Jamaica
Inn

Sons of Jamaica Inn

by

Jill Batters

Best Wishes

Jill Batters

The majority of this novel is based on true facts connected with the Jamaica Inn, to which certain names, characters and incidents have been added from the author's imagination.

Apart from the true facts, any resemblance to actual persons, living or dead, events or locations is entirely coincidental.

Published by: CB Productions (Cornwall)
Bodmin, Cornwall. PL31 2AR

Printed and bound by
TJ International Ltd. of Padstow, Cornwall.

Cover design by Aidan Booth

ISBN – 978-0-9569189-3-2

This book is dedicated to my
husband Chris for his continual
encouragement and assistance, and to
our two dogs Oliver and Charlie for their constant
company during my many hours of writing.

By the same author & publisher

'From the Vision to the Noose'

*A true 1840's Cornish story of murder
and intrigue, the victim of the crime being the
great-grandfather of the famous novelist
Neville Shute*

ISBN – 978-0-9569189-0-1

Also by Jill Batters

'The Life of Charlotte Dymond'

*Flesh on the bones of this true Cornish murder
story from the 1800's. Secrets and jealousy collide
to doubly fulfil the tragic prophesy.
Two young lives are cut short before their time.*

ISBN – 978-0-9569189-2-5

Jill Batters – Cornish Author

Jill Batters is a Cornish born writer living in Bodmin.
'Sons of Jamaica Inn' is Jill's third novel.

All three of Jill's books are set in the Cornwall of the past and are recognised as being well written accounts of life in bye-gone days.

'Sons of Jamaica Inn' is a story that starts in Jamaica and returns to Cornwall, covering a period of over two hundred and fifty years of life on the magnificent Bodmin Moor.
The story also covers the Trelawny family and the Cornish fishing town of Looe, with its rugged coastline.

Smuggling, intrigue and the history of the famous Trelawny family are all part of this superbly written novel.

Chapter One

November 1742

From her bedroom window at King's House in Port Royal, on the southern coast of Jamaica, Annabelle Trelawny could see her cousin Edward sitting by himself in the gardens below her. It was a rare moment, as Edward never relaxed outside in the gardens. And he was alone! A rare moment indeed! Now was the time to talk to him; tell him how she really felt about her life in this damnable place. It had to be done. It was regrettable though that she would be disturbing him, as the poor man had very little time to himself.

As the British Governor of Jamaica, appointed four years earlier in the April of 1738, he had from the start, immersed himself almost totally in his work. It had therefore been a wise decision, made by his family, in the weeks before he left England in the winter of 1737, to send Annabelle to Jamaica with him as a companion for his young wife, Amoretta. The couple, both born into ancient and well known Cornish families, had married in the autumn of that same year, just before they were due to set sail to distant shores, and it was clear to everyone who knew them that they loved each other dearly. The bride's family were very happy with their union, despite the fact that Amoretta, or Amy as she was always known, had only recently celebrated her twentieth birthday, and Edward his thirty-ninth. They did, however, voice concerns for Amy on two accounts; firstly, that her health had always been quite delicate; and secondly, that she was a rather reserved young woman who did not take easily to strangers.

After some discussion between them and Edward's family, who were equally concerned, it had been Annabelle herself who had suggested that she should accompany the couple to Jamaica. It was, she'd said, the obvious solution to the problem. As an unmarried, middle aged woman of independent means, who'd spent most of her life living with family members, either in London or in Cornwall, she had no ties, and was always ready for adventure.

"If Amy can put up with a middle aged spinster as a companion in Jamaica, then I will be more than happy to set sail with them!" she'd said.
But sadly there had been very little happiness to be found in Jamaica for the Trelawny family.

Her suggestion had been readily accepted by everyone concerned, especially by Amy, and in the April of 1738 the Trelawnys had arrived in Port Royal, on board the naval frigate HMS Endurance, to start their new life together. Edward had taken office as the Governor of an island where the economy depended mostly on the success of its sugar plantations, and therefore on slavery. Many thousands of African people had been, for more than two hundred years, bought or captured and taken from their own country to work in Jamaica on the sugar plantations. Conditions on board the ships that carried them away from their homes and their families were so horrific that most of them died on the journey. Of those that survived, almost half of them died within the following three years.

In the past the island had belonged to Spain, but in 1655, when the British took Jamaica from the Spanish, many slaves fled to the mountains, to areas where it was almost impossible for their owners to find them.

The trade in slaves from Africa continued and by the time that Edward Trelawny took over as the Governor of Jamaica, a state of war had existed between the English settlers and the escaped slaves, now named Maroons, for several generations. Many thousands of Maroon warriors lived in the mountains, and these descendants of former slaves, naturally welcomed any runaway slaves into their midst.

Edward soon discovered that the English plantation owners wanted an end to this escape route for their slaves, and an end to the war with the Maroons, and so he set about establishing a peace agreement

between them. This had been completed on the 1st March, 1739. The Maroons were officially given their freedom and the English settlers gave them land where they could live on separate reservations, and govern themselves. However, one of the conditions imposed upon these proud people caused a rift between them. They were required to return any future runaway slaves to the plantation. For this they would be paid for each and every slave, but as they did not all agree with this, it naturally caused further unrest on the island.
Privately Edward saw this peace treaty as a victory; his first step towards the abolition of the slave trade. Personally, he wished to see slavery abolished altogether, but since that would have ruined the economy of the island, he knew that this was, for the time being, an impossible dream. Edward was not alone in his thorough dislike of this trade in slaves. There were periods of time when Annabelle herself had been almost obsessed by it.

Edward was looking at his pocket watch, tapping the glass as if he thought that time was somehow standing still. Annabelle hurried out of her room, hoping to catch him before he returned to the house and to his duties as Governor. To reach the stairs she had to pass the door to the nursery, the little room that had been made ready, twelve months earlier, for a very precious occupant, Edward and Amy's newborn child. Sadly, the little room had never heard that child cry, or listened to its laughter. Amy had died in the November of 1741, whilst giving birth to a baby boy who had only survived his mother by two days. They were buried together in the graveyard at St Catherine's Church, and buried with them was Annabelle's sole reason for being on the island. Longing to be in England again, to walk on Cornish soil and be with a family that she loved, she began to feel that she was herself a prisoner in a country where she could not escape the constant reminders of the horrors of slavery.

On Edward's instruction, the door to the nursery had been locked, its key put away, and, for the past twelve months, Annabelle had cast her eyes to the floor and tiptoed past that room, as if she were afraid that she may somehow disturb a sleeping ghost.

Today something was very different. As Annabelle approached the nursery door she could see that it was open; someone was inside the room. Peering in through the door, she was shocked to find two women servants folding bedding and baby clothes, packing them away into a small trunk in the corner of the room.
"Does the Governor know that you are in this room?"
Her voice was barely audibly but one of the women turned, and seeing the dismay on Annabelle's face, hurried over to her side.
"Oh Madam! The Governor has said nothing to you of this? He asked that we clear the room, but we will leave it for a while if you wish to speak to him….."
The woman's words petered away, but her eyes were full of sorrow.

“No, no. Please continue with your work, Hessy. I’m sure the Governor has his reasons. As it happens I am on my way to see him now.”

As the two women nodded and solemnly returned to their tasks, Annabelle quickly left them, but on the turn of the stairs she was further angered to see Edward striding down the hallway towards his office.
“Edward!” She called out to him, but, seemingly oblivious to everything around him, he entered his room and firmly closed the door.

Annabelle stormed into the office and threw herself down into the comfortable chair behind the large oak desk. Edward’s chair.
“Damn it, Edward. Why wasn’t I told about the nursery?”

He was standing by the long window, looking out into the courtyard. Slowly he turned to look at her and was surprised to see her trembling slightly. Annabelle was a strong woman, his elder by less than twelve months and they had always been close. His childhood memories were mostly happy ones; loving parents, ten brothers and sisters, and Annabelle, always Annabelle, guiding him through the trials of his early life; his life before he had left the family home to attend Westminster school. And he would never forget his cousin’s struggle to keep his infant son alive; nursing him day and night. Sadly they had all lost that battle. Annabelle had been the perfect choice as a companion for Amy, successfully helping to ease his young wife into her new role beside her husband, the new Governor of Jamaica.

"I'm sorry Edward. I didn't come here to speak about the nursery. It was a shock that's all. It's been a year now and I admit it will be easier to pass the room if it is empty or used for some other purpose. But we could have discussed it Edward, surely."
"It was a decision that I made only this morning, Annabelle. I didn't expect the servants to act on it quite so soon. I should have spoken with you first of course, but I have been making quite a lot of decisions lately my dear, some of which do involve you."

She was looking concerned now, her normally wide grey eyes narrowed slightly.

"Edward, I sought you out today to insist that you put me on the first available ship back to England. There is no joy for me now living here at King's House without Amy. You are working day in and day out and I hardly ever see you. On the rare occasions that you do need me, to go with you to a dinner party on a sugar plantation, I am made miserable by the company of people who use these poor African slaves in the way that they do. I despise not being able to speak out; tell them how I feel about their slave trade!"
"But I need you at these dinner parties, Annabelle. Your presence there helps to fend off the attentions

of all those husband hungry ladies who are deliberately seated so close to me."
He was smiling now. Dear Annabelle. She found it hard when she couldn't speak her mind. The truth was that she had always been far too outspoken for her own good, and this, coupled with her preference for gin over the rather more acceptable beverages, had frightened off many a good suitor over the years.
"Edward, I will not be trifled with over this. If you have better reasons for needing me here then I will stay. But I have been thinking recently of the happiness that you found with Amy. I would like to find such happiness for myself Edward. There may still be someone waiting for me back home, someone as unconventional as myself perhaps, someone who doesn't have to mix in those oh so polite circles of society."

Edward knew he would miss his favourite cousin if she returned to England, but he also knew that she deserved much more than he could offer her now. As Governor, he could possibly be in Jamaica for many more years, and poor Annabelle seemed to thoroughly despise living on the island. Now in her early forties she was still a fine looking woman, with those large grey eyes, a generous smile, and her pale gold hair, which she always wore piled untidily on the top of her head.
"I realised some time ago Annabelle, that you wished to return home, but I knew that I would not be able to live with myself if I just sent you away on the first available ship, as you so carelessly put it.

These sea journeys are perilous enough for any traveller, but for a woman alone, on a ship with a captain and a crew that I knew nothing about? I would have never even contemplated it Annabelle, you must know that. But, that said, I believe I may now have a solution to our problem; if, that is, you are agreeable to the plans that I have made."
He paused, waiting for a smile, some sign of approval, but she was frowning at him, her mouth pursed.
"Please continue Edward. Tell me of these plans that you have made, once more without consulting me. And how long may I ask will it be before I can see England again?"
"Annabelle, do you remember the Stewart family from Saltsprings on the north coast of the island? We dined there with Amy sometime last year."

"I do. Of course I do." She was still frowning. "They had a large family, nine daughters I believe and one son. Seemed unusually sympathetic towards their slaves, as I remember. And there was a young captain from the merchant service, an Alex Stewart, I believe, a distant relative from Scotland. Very taken with the eldest daughter and she with him. But what has this to do with me, Edward?"
"You're right my dear. The young couple were very taken with each other. In fact, so much so that when he returns to Jamaica this April, they are to marry. I received a letter from the Stewarts only last week with an invitation, which includes you Annabelle, to the wedding. Soon after the wedding, Megan Stewart will sail back to England with her husband. I

understand that they plan to live in London where the young captain already has a house of his own. I sent a reply to Iain Stewart and his wife, accepting their invitation on behalf of us both, and asking if it would be possible for you to sail with them Annabelle. I am afraid that I acted again without consulting you, but I felt it best to at least enquire, before giving you any false hopes of a safe return to England. They have replied to me my dear; the letter arrived early this morning, stating that, not only will you be able to travel with them, but that Megan will be delighted to have a female friend for company, someone that she knows well!"

"But Edward, Megan doesn't know me at all well. We exchanged a few words at that dinner party but I can scarcely remember what the girl looks like!"
"The Stewarts have asked if you would be willing to stay with them for a while Annabelle, in fact for as long as you wish. Apparently they are all looking forward to spending some time with you, before the ship sets sail for England."
"This is against the grain, Edward! Why can't the girl come here to visit with us? You really can't expect me to stay on a sugar plantation; live in such close contact with the owners of slaves!"
"Annabelle!"

Suddenly she was smiling. Unpredictable as ever.
"Well I have been thinking lately Edward, that I would do *anything* to go home again. You may reply that I will accept their invitation. But only for a short while you understand. If I am to travel with Megan,

then we should get to know each other better. And I have to consider your peace of mind Edward. You are confident that I will not fall into the hands of pirates, or go down with the ship in a hurricane?" She was goading him now, her grey eyes narrow; her manner brisk.
"I cannot be sure of anything my dear, you know that. But it is my guess that the young captain will not take any unnecessary risks; not with the woman he loves on board his ship!"

It was a warm day in February, at Saltspings dry weather estate in Hanover Parish, County Cornwall, Jamaica. Situated as it was on the coastline, conditions were perfect for the growing of sugar cane. One third of the estate was given over to sugar and corn, and the remainder to pasture and woodland.

In the early afternoon sunshine, two women walked companionably together around the outskirts of that woodland, their arms linked as they made their way back to the house. From somewhere far away, deep inside the little forest of trees, the sound of excited voices broke out, cutting sharply in across the relaxing sense of peace that had surrounded the plantation that afternoon.

"They are felling some of the trees. It is dangerous work but the men seem to enjoy it."
Megan Stewart glanced nervously at the woman by her side. They had grown close to each other over the past weeks, but Annabelle Trelawny had not

been able to hide her distaste for Jamaica's trade in slaves. As it was the only bone of contention between them, Megan did her best to avoid the subject, or when she could not, to convince the older woman that the slaves on her father's estate were treated well and seemed, for the most part, content with their lives. But as she waited for the next caustic remark from her new friend, they were both startled by the sound of something crashing through the undergrowth in the woodland just behind them. Anxiously looking around, they were relieved to see a small boy emerge from the edge of the trees and turn to run towards them. He was staggering slightly, leaning forward as he ran, his dark eyes fixed on them until he stopped, just a few paces away on the path and then, as those eyes rolled upwards, he cried out and fell to the ground, almost at their feet.

"Tombar! What has happened? Can you hear me?"
Megan knelt down beside the boy and took his hand.
"Who is this child?" Annabelle hovered over them anxiously.
"He lives with the servants, but he is a slave, Annabelle. Wake up Tombar! What is wrong with you?"
Megan put one arm under the boy's shoulders, trying to lift him, and then she saw the blood, dripping from a large wound on the right side of his head, already staining the earth beneath him.
"He's badly injured, Megan. We have to get him back to the house. We'll lift him together. Carry him back if we have to. Tombar! Is that his name? Can

you hear me Tombar? We are going to take you home."
The boy groaned, opened his eyes and somehow struggled to his feet.
"Can you walk? If he can walk, Megan, we could support him between us. But he must not fall asleep. We must keep him awake."

They walked together slowly with their own arms hooked under his, holding him so that his feet touched the ground, while they carried most of his weight.
"Keep walking, Tombar. You must stay awake. He does understand me doesn't he, Megan? He can speak English?"
"He has been brought up speaking English. His mother was expecting him when she arrived in Jamaica on a slave ship. My father knew nothing of it when he bought her to work on the plantation, but when Tombar was born he gave him to the servants to be cared for while his mother was working. She looked after him at night, of course, but Tombar was only two years old when she died of a fever. Our servants brought him up then, all of them watching out for him as if he were their own."
"Surely he was not working in the woodland today. He looks far too small. Do you know how old he is Megan?"
"He is working with the men now, Annabelle. He turned eight years of age this year."
"He looks so fragile." Annabelle looked down at the boy. He was fighting so hard just to put one foot in front of the other, trying not to fall asleep.

“Well done, Tombar. Keep walking. I will tell you a story to help you stay awake.” And she went on to tell him that while his home in Jamaica was by the sea in a county named Cornwall, her home, far away in England was also by the sea in the county of Cornwall. To keep him awake she tried to paint vivid pictures in his mind of a land where there were no slaves, and of Trelawne, the manor house where she had spent such happy times when she was a child.

“My family own a lot of land in Cornwall, Tombar,” she told him, “but we do not own the people who live and work on our land. They are there because that is what they have chosen to do. They are free men and women. I am returning to England soon, sailing back with Miss Megan and her Captain Stewart after their wedding. God willing I shall be at home in Cornwall for the best part of our warmest season, and with my family to celebrate the end of the harvest.”

As their little trio drew near to the house, they were spotted from the yard by one of the male servants, who straightaway ran out to meet them. Taking Tombar from them, he placed the boy over his shoulder and hurried away towards the servants’ quarters, leaving Annabelle and Megan to follow at their own pace. Apart from crying out when he had fallen at their feet on the path beside the woodland, Tombar had remained silent throughout his ordeal. But from his lofty position on the young servant’s shoulder, his liquid brown eyes met Annabelle’s, and spoke volumes, thanking her far more than any words that he may have been able to utter.

Chapter Two

May 1743

As a privileged passenger on board Captain Stewart's merchant ship The White Whale, Annabelle had been given her own small cabin. Available space was limited, but in her trunk, stored away under the narrow bed, she had been able to pack some of her clothes, her Bible, and basic provisions for the trip. Amongst these basic provisions were several bottles and a flask, all containing her favourite tipple of gin; much needed liquid sustenance for a long and dangerous journey, and giving far more comfort than the tasteless tea or weak coffee that would have been on offer from the ship's provisions.

The White Whale was only two days out of Port Royal, and already pitching in rough seas; an unexpected storm sending its passengers below deck to their cabins, and its crew to firmly secure the hatchways.

Annabelle, sitting alone on her bed, consoled herself with the knowledge that unlike the violent storms which would rage around the Caribbean ocean in the hurricane season between June and September, this storm in early May would be no real threat to their safety. Nevertheless, as the groaning ship battled against the howling wind, Annabelle threw herself to her knees on the floor of the dark cabin, to rummage in the bag at the bottom of the trunk, for that much needed flask of gin. The constant rocking of the ship made standing difficult, but somehow Annabelle managed to regain her seat on the narrow bed. A sudden urgent knocking on her cabin door almost caused her to choke on the swig of precious liquid that she'd taken from the flask.

"Miss Trelawny. Can I come in? I need your assistance." It was Alex Stewart at her cabin door. There was no mistaking his voice.

"Whatever is wrong Captain Stewart? Is it Megan? Has something happened to Megan?"

"No, no it's not Megan. Two of my men have found a stowaway in the cargo hold. They should have left him there until we were out of the storm, but they brought him to me. I would ask Megan, Miss Trelawny, but she is suffering greatly with sea sickness."

"The door is not locked Captain. You may come in. But what I can do to help you with a stowaway is beyond me."

As the cabin door opened and the Captain stepped through into her little room, Annabelle's hands flew to her face, causing some of the contents of her flask to spill out onto her skirts. For into the room with the Captain came Tombar, standing proudly but trembling; held only by the collar of his shirt.

“This is our stowaway, Miss Trelawny. The boy has been saying that he knows you. That he has run away from Saltsprings to travel to England with you.”

“I wish to live in your Cornwall, Miss Annabelle. I wish to work on your estate, and to be free.”

“Well Tombar. What am I to do with you? I do know this boy Alex, as does your Megan, though this is the first time that I have heard him speak. He will be safe here with me for now. I am sure that you need to return to your crew.”

“You have my gratitude, Miss Trelawny.” Alex Stewart turned away, and holding firmly onto the frame of the cabin door stepped out into the passageway, closing the door behind him. Young Tombar watched in awe as Annabelle retrieved her flask and slowly drank it dry.

And so as one storm ended out at sea that May in 1743, another began.

Whilst Megan was adamant that Tombar should be returned to her father’s plantation at Saltspings, Annabelle was equally adamant that he should be allowed to live with her in England.

“He belongs to my father, Annabelle. When we reach North America, he must be put aboard the first ship that is sailing back to Jamaica. Whichever way you look at it, he is still a slave, a stowaway who has not paid for his passage.”

“I will pay his passage, Megan. And if necessary, although it galls me to say it, I will buy Tombar from your father and then grant him his freedom.

When we reach North America I will send letters back to Jamaica, both to Edward and to your father, explaining all of this. I am quite sure that they will allow the boy to stay with me. Your father may have bought Tombar's mother, Megan, but he did not buy the boy. You told me yourself that he knew nothing of any unborn child until after Tombar's birth. And since his mother lived and worked as your father's slave for more than two years, I am sure that he would not have thought himself cheated out of his money when the poor woman died."

Their battle of words raged on until Alex Stewart intervened and suggested that if Tombar worked his passage, he would agree to let him sail back to England with them. Tired of their bickering, he told them that he would do his best to sort out their predicament when they all reached London. In the meantime he said that he hoped that they could forget their differences; leave him in peace to carry out his duties, and return his ship safely to shore.

"I must admit that I am not happy when we disagree, Annabelle. I am hoping that we can continue to be friends when I am living in London."

"My dear girl. I have both family and friends in London. If your husband will allow me, I intend to introduce you to them all and to ask them to take you under their wing when he returns to sea."

"And Tombar?" asked Megan, "what will they say when you introduce them to Tombar?"

"They will say that the rather eccentric Annabelle Trelawny has returned from Jamaica, with a slave in tow, a runaway child who stowed away on a ship to be with her. But they will whisper it behind their hands my dear. They will not dare to say it to my face."

They had been in London for less than a month when a letter arrived from Edward, informing them that Iain Stewart had agreed to let Tombar remain in England with Annabelle, and that he had officially granted him his freedom. Edward wrote that Megan's father wished them all well and was asking, on behalf of the house servants at Saltsprings, that they send news of the boy from time to time.

With Tombar's future settled, Annabelle soon found that she was longing for the sanity of Trelawne Manor and Cornwall. For the first time in her life she felt suffocated by the very same family and friends whose company she had always enjoyed in those now long gone years before Jamaica and the hell of slavery. Tombar had been made welcome in London. As a little black African child, a runaway slave, a stowaway aboard The White Whale, he had become the latest topic of conversation; something of a curiosity. Annabelle Trelawny, along with the boy, Megan Stewart and her affable Captain had become the ones to invite around for afternoon tea; valuable companions at the dinner table.

As soon as it became clear that Megan was settling happily into her new life in England, and would be cared for during Iain Stewart's frequent journeys away from home, Annabelle made arrangements to return to the sanctuary of the only place that she had ever really thought of as her home. Orphaned as a small child, she'd grown up knowing little about herself, except for the all-important fact that she was a Trelawny. Her father, a William Trelawny, had been the rector of a small church somewhere in Wiltshire. He had married an Ann Bell, the second daughter of a wealthy merchant, and they had named their little daughter Annabelle, for her mother and for the Bell family. Sadly Ann had died at a very young age, leaving William alone to bring up his daughter to the tender age of three and a half years when he was also taken from her as he stood nearby to his church, awaiting his congregation on a Sunday morning; killed instantly by a runaway coach and horses.

Left comfortably off by her parents and well provided for by the Bell family, little Annabelle had been raised mostly by the well-meaning Trelawny family, who had chosen to share her out between themselves. Consequently she was moved about every few months, to be treated well by new faces at differing places of residence, until the day that she arrived at Trelawne in Cornwall for the first time, and stole the hearts of the most well-known Trelawny family in England.

Jonathan Trelawny had been born at Trelawne Manor in the parish of Pelynt in 1650. Educated at Oxford he became a clergyman; the rector of South Hill and of St Ive in Cornwall in 1677.

In 1685, when the Duke of Monmouth rose up in the west, against King James II, Jonathan helped his elder brother, Major General Charles Trelawny to put down the rebellion, thus earning himself the name of Christian Turk. The King rewarded him well for his services, making him the Bishop of Bristol, in the November of 1685.

When his father and his brother Charles died, Jonathan inherited both title and estates as the third Baronet, and became Sir Jonathan Trelawny.
He fell in love with, and married Rebeka Hele and they started their family. But in 1687, the same year that their daughter Charlotte was born, Jonathan found himself torn between his God and his King when James II introduced his Declaration of Indulgence, which granted religious tolerance to the Catholics. When the King commanded that his Declaration was to be read out in all churches throughout the land, Sir Jonathan and six other bishops refused, and were imprisoned in the Tower of London for their rebellion. Their belief that their duty towards God should be greater than their duty towards their King, led to a trial, but they were acquitted and the Cornish people celebrated the return of one of their County's favourite sons.

Soon after this, and around the time that Sir Jonathan's second daughter Letitia was born, William of Orange, the Protestant son-in-law of James II landed in England, bringing with him an invasion army from the Netherlands. Church leaders and politicians no longer trusted James, a staunch Catholic who was suspected of being pro-French. They, including Sir Jonathan Trelawny, supported William, and James fled England, to be succeeded by his Protestant daughter Mary and her husband William. It was after this that Sir Jonathan was appointed Bishop of Exeter.

For Rebeka Trelawny, holding baby Hele in her arms as she laid eyes on five year old Annabelle for the first time, the decision was easy. The little girl with pale untidy hair and a big smile had to stay with her at Trelawne and become part of the family. The bedrooms at the manor house were already filling up with their nine surviving children; one more would make no difference.

Growing up, belonging, but never quite belonging anywhere, Annabelle continued to visit her other cousins around the country. For whatever reason, she seemed to possess an in-built desire to move on from time to time, despite the fact that she was happiest at Trelawne, her only real home.

Although two of her cousins, Elizabeth and Rebecka were close to her in age, it was young Edward who became her dearest friend. Her fondest childhood memories always took her back to Trelawne in the summertime; long warm days when she would wander around the estate with Edward, sometimes even walking through the woods to the bottom of the hill and the banks of the river at West Looe.

A few days before Annabelle and Tombar were to leave London for Cornwall, the family received the sad news that Rebecka Trelawny had died. Just three years older than Annabelle, she had married, at the age of twenty one, into the Buller family, and left her home at Trelawne. Happily married to John Buller, she had borne him thirteen children. Since five of her children were still living at home when their mother died, Rebecka's two unmarried sisters, Charlotte and Ann, had offered their support, and were leaving Trelawne to stay with their four nieces and eight year old William over the summer months.

Annabelle was heartbroken. Well over twenty years had passed since she had lost her Aunt Rebeka and Uncle Jonathon, and almost three years since, whilst in Jamaica, she'd received the news that Hele, who was some five years her junior, had also died. And now Rebecka had been taken from them. But, for Tombar, she kept smiling. The boy was so excited to, at last, be going to Cornwall.

"We'll have Trelawne to ourselves Tombar. Just the two of us and the servants. They will love you, I am sure of it. We'll have them make up a bedroom for you and then we'll spend our days doing anything and everything that we wish to do. How would you like that?"

"What work will I do at Trelawne, Miss Annabelle? I could help the servants in the house, or work outside on your farm."

It seemed that Tombar wanted to start work as soon as they arrived on the estate.

"I will need you to do something for me at first Tombar. I will need a companion, so that I do not get lonely there without my cousins. This will be your work until my cousins come home. They will know where you will be needed the most."

And so, as Tombar worked for his Miss Annabelle at the ancestral home of the Trelawny's, she told him everything that she knew of their history. As they wandered through the attic rooms in the roof space of the manor; searching for a bedroom that Tombar could make his own, he learned that the Trelawny family had been landowners and lived in a mansion on the bleak moorland between Bodmin and Launceston, some twenty miles inland from Trelawne. The mansion had long been dismantled, but the family still owned land and farmhouses out on the moors.

Warm days were spent in the gardens near to the house, sitting lazily by the lily ponds, cooling themselves beside the intriguing water fountains. In the walled courtyard at the back of the house they could hide from the rest of the world, breathing in the fragrance from herbs and bright flowers; watching white doves strutting on the grass around their feet, or flying high above them, though never quite out of sight.

On cooler days they picked apples in the small orchard or walked down through the woods to the river, much as Annabelle had done in her younger days with Edward. There were also the small farms

to explore; farms that were attached to the manor, tenanted by farmers who also worked, when they were needed, on the home farm.
The crops were standing tall, almost ready to bring in, and as Tombar watched the workers preparing for the long exhausting task ahead of them, his excitement was growing. He had been asked to help with the harvest, and Miss Annabelle had agreed that it was time for him to start his work on the estate.

She had received a letter from an elderly aunt on her mother's side of her family. The old lady had only recently learned that Annabelle had returned to Cornwall from Jamaica and was urging her niece to visit with her, before the winter set in. That letter aroused the restless spirit that had lain dormant, somewhere deep inside her, for a brief but happy time.

Charlotte and Ann were coming back to Trelawne for the harvest. When the weather had been kind, it was the best time of the year on any farm. For master and servant alike, bringing in the wheat crop at the end of the summer, drew everyone closer together, and Annabelle was hoping that for Tombar, labouring alongside the men and women who worked on her cousin Edward's estate, the harvest would once again work its magic and her little stowaway would know that he belonged in England, in Cornwall and there at Trelawne. She would spend some time with her returning cousins and then travel for a while, leaving Tombar under their watchful eyes and where, it seemed, he most wanted to be.

It was late morning and they were in the orchard, taking some of the best apples from the trees for Cook to make a pie for their meal in the evening.
"Mrs Clemo makes the best pies that I have ever tasted." Annabelle was arranging the apples in a basket, covering them with a cloth to keep the wasps away as Tombar appeared at her side. He was grinning; carrying more rosy apples wrapped up in the front of his shirt.
"I met Cook's husband this morning," he said. "He came into the kitchen when I was having something to eat. He asked me why you haven't taken me to see his farm. He said it's the nearest farm to the manor, and that if we call in there later on today, there'll be a slice of cake and a jug of goat's milk ready for us on the table. Can we go, Miss Annabelle? He said it's the best farm on the whole estate, except for the home farm of course, and Cook said that you'd never been there, not even when you were young, and she's been living there for thirty years, so she should know." He tipped the apples into the basket as Annabelle removed the cover, and stood watching her patiently, waiting for an answer.
"The basket's full now Tombar," she said quietly. "You should take them to Cook. I think I'll stay indoors this afternoon, my head is aching a little. Too much sun perhaps. But you can go to Cook's farm today. Now that you've met Reg Clemo, you can go there on your own. He's a good man, Tombar. Cook is always talking about him. Now take these to the kitchen and we'll have our apple pie together later."

Annabelle watched the boy as he strolled away, loose limbed and sure footed, holding the basket in his arms.

Wearily she followed him into the manor house and climbed the main staircase, absentmindedly trailing her hand across each twisted pillar below the ornamental handrail. Searching a large trunk in her bedroom, she found her flask of gin and sank down on the comfortable bed before opening it.
Thirty years! Such an age since she had last set foot on what was now the Clemo's farm. And she knew herself, far better than Cook knew, that it had been at this exact time of year, not long before the harvest, that her son had been conceived right there, in the cottage on that very farm. He would be thirty years old in the spring, on the second of April, and while she prayed that he had survived and would soon reach that age, she was ashamed that she had never once tried to find out if he were alive or dead.

She had been just fifteen years of age, returning to Trelawne in the early June of 1713 to discover that Edward was no longer there. He had been sent away to school in Westminster earlier in the year and would not be returning home for several weeks. Bored without her dearest friend for company, she had felt compelled to spend her time in the house with her uncle and those of her cousins who were for various reasons living at Trelawne that summer.

Her dear aunt Rebecca had died three years earlier, and since then her uncle Jonathon had spent much of his time at Trelawne, despite having been made the Bishop of Winchester in 1707, in the same year that his youngest child Ann had been born.

Looking for ways to amuse herself, she had made it a pastime to sit in the chair beside her bedroom window. From there she'd been able to look out over the cobbled courtyard at the back of the house, beside the kitchen. For an hour or two after first light she had watched the servants arrive, apparently eager to make a start on their day's work, bustling about and disturbing the old house, room by room, until, rudely woken from restful slumber, it was ready to greet the day.

Not many days had passed by though before she'd realised that there was in truth, just one man that she was watching for. He would turn up at varying times on varying days, but always with the same horse and cart, always wearing the same worn out waistcoat and cloth cap. Stopping below her bedroom window he would roll up his shirt sleeves, climb down from the front of the cart and walk around to the back to begin unloading wooden box after wooden box, all filled to the brim with potatoes, carrots, turnips or greens, which he would then carry off, one box at a time into the kitchen. He would be joined, almost straight away, by one of the kitchen maids, a pretty, lively girl with dark hair who would flirt with him as they laughed together, searching for a light box for her to carry. She'd always walked ahead of him as they carried the boxes into the house, swaying her

hips and smiling back over her shoulder, encouraging him.
When the cart was emptied she would follow him from the kitchen and they would linger there for a while, talking, sometimes touching, their eyes locked together, until one morning, watching from her bedroom window, she'd found herself envying that kitchen maid and wishing beyond anything she had ever wished for before, that he would look at her and laugh with her in that way.

Leaving her chair she'd moved across the window, trying to properly see his face. Somehow he had seen that movement and, looking up at her standing there to the side of the window, he'd removed his cap and given her a little mock bow before turning all of his attention back to the maid.

He'd had a handsome face, thick, red brown hair, drowsy amused eyes, and she had loved him, as only a silly fifteen year old girl could love someone that she didn't know in any way at all. Asking questions about him, offhand but guarded questions that had aroused no suspicions; she'd learned that his name was Jake Allen, and that he was living with his wife in the cottage on the nearest farm that was attached to the estate.

They'd soon tired of being watched, Jake Allen and his kitchen maid. He'd found somewhere else to leave his horse and cart in the mornings, well away from prying eyes. She'd walked about the estate then; spent days just looking for him, though never daring to walk too close to his fields or his cottage.

One morning though as she'd been returning to the manor and passing the old, unused gatehouse, she'd heard voices inside. Charlotte had mentioned to her, some days before, that her cousin Charles would be coming back to Trelawne to live for a while. He'd been up at Oxford for the past year, but they had received a letter from him, saying that he'd not been well for some time and that he would like, if at all possible, to make the old gatehouse his home for a while on his return. Charlotte had laughed.
'Four years away at school and one at Oxford' she'd said, *'and now he's pining for his home, but reluctant to give up his independence it seems.'*

The door to the gatehouse had been open and she'd found four of the servants downstairs, in what had been the kitchen.
'We're to do it up, Miss,' one of the women had told her, *'make it fit for Mr Charles to come here to live. There's rooms up above, as well as servants' rooms down here.'*
And then he'd come running down over the stairs, straight into the kitchen. Jake Allen.
'It's a fine house,' he'd said, *'I'd like the chance to live here myself!'*
He'd smiled at her, nodded before he'd walked away into another room, but after that she'd known where to find him. She visited them in the gatehouse on most days, making a nuisance of herself no doubt, but she'd also spent hours outside, sitting on a low

wall to look in through the windows and watch him while he worked away inside.

One very warm afternoon though he'd surprised her, coming out of the kitchen to sit beside her on the wall.

'What are you doing here, Miss?' he'd asked. *'They've been laughing in there, saying you're sweet on me.'*

'Well what if I am?' She hadn't denied it. *'There's no harm in just watching someone, is there?'*

'No harm, Miss, but I'm married, and if my Kath should get wind of it, well she might get it into her head that I've encouraged you.'

'But you haven't. In fact you've hidden from me; especially in the mornings. But I think, Jake Allen, that you've encouraged our kitchen maid. What if your Kath gets wind of that?'

He'd looked straight at her; seemed shocked at her bold words.

'That was different, Miss. We were just larking about. I told her though, after I saw you watching us. Told her I didn't need her help with the vegetables no more. I don't want people talking and I don't want my Kath upset. She's not herself right now; me neither for that matter. So if you could stay away Miss I'd be obliged. The work's near finished anyways. I'll tell the others that you're just lonely with Mr Edward away. Nothing to do but watch us work. They'll know that's right.'

'It's true I've missed Edward this summer.' She'd been surprised that he'd known of her friendship with her young cousin.

'We watch what's going on with you and the family, Miss. Same as you watch us. No harm in that.'
He'd winked at her before going back into the kitchen. He shouldn't have winked at her.

Two or three days had passed before Charlotte had asked her to take a message to the servants' quarters.
'Annabelle my dear,' she'd said, as they'd met in the upstairs corridor, beside the library door.
'What a blessing. Could you find a servant who will go to the gatehouse for me and tell whoever is there that the house must be ready at the end of the day. Charles will be here tomorrow, sometime in the morning. Would you do that for me dear? I really haven't the time to spend on it myself. Your uncle is expecting a visit from two old friends within the hour and I must be with him to greet them.'

'Oh, I'll not trouble the servants Charlotte,' she'd said. *'I'll go there for you myself.'*

There had been only two people working in the gatehouse that morning. Two men, who had nodded as she'd given them the message from Charlotte.
'The work's been held up Miss Annabelle,' one of them had said, *'but the place will be ready by nightfall. The last of the furniture should be here in an hour or so. We'd have been finished before now, but we had to find someone to fetch it. I'd asked Jake Allen to go for it, but he forgot. Turned up here*

this morning without his horse and cart, and not feeling too good, so I sent him back home.'

'Not feeling too good! Is that what you call it? Too drunk to stand up straight is more like the truth of it!' The younger man had scoffed at his words, starting an argument.

'You mind your tongue in front of the lady young, Sam,' the older man had said. *'Jake's troubles are none of your business. I've sent him back to his farm and his wife will take care of him. He'll be right as rain tomorrow.'*
'Well his wife's not there. Gone off to her sister's in Looe for the day he told me. Seems she can't bear to watch him when he's drinking himself senseless. He'd have been better off staying here if you ask me. State he was in he won't make it back to that cottage of his.'

She'd left them to their disagreement and headed straightaway for Jake's farm. The door to the kitchen had been wide open and she'd walked in, calling his name softly, just the once, *'Jake.'*

'Kath? Is that you?' He'd answered her from upstairs and she'd climbed up over those stairs; found him sitting on the edge of a low bed, holding his head in one hand and a bottle of gin in the other. He'd looked up at her, his eyes half closed and his skin flushed.
'I thought you were my Kath.'

She'd tried to explain. *'I was worried. They said at the gatehouse that you were ill, that you'd been drinking and your wife was not at home to look after you.'*

'No need for you to bother yourself over us Miss Annabelle,' he'd said. *'I'm grieving and Kath's grieving and this is our way. I drink and she can't stand to watch me, so she goes off to her sister's place. She'll be back tomorrow and we'll be alright again. You go back to your manor house Miss and leave me alone to finish this.'* He'd held up the half empty bottle before starting to drink from it again. She should have turned away and left him then; gone down over those stairs and walked back to her own life, but instead she had lowered herself down to sit beside him on the bed. She had needed to know.
'Why are you grieving?' she'd asked and, after what had seemed like an age, he had answered her.
'We lost our boy. Just two years old he was. Hair as white as the snow. Sturdy and strong. He died though. Five years back on this very day. And there's been no sign of any more youngsters for us.'

She'd reached out to touch him, comfort him, but he'd pulled away from her.
'Leave me be, Miss Annabelle. You can't know what it's like, so just leave me be.'
'You are right,' she'd said. *'It is true that I don't know what it's like for you. You have lost a child. But I was a child when I lost my parents. My mother died first and then my father when I was just three years old and too young even to remember him. I*

have had nothing of them to carry with me through my life, so I do know what it is like to grieve, Jake Allen.'

He had turned to her then, holding her, kissing her face, and she had kissed him back, again and again until he had fallen back on the bed and drawn her down beside him. He had loved her so sweetly, so very gently, but when it was over he had moved away to sit on the edge of the bed again, looking back at her as he picked up the bottle of gin from the floor. She hadn't understood why he had left her. *'Come back to me Jake,'* she'd said. *'Lie with me again.'*
'We can never breathe a word of this,' he'd said. *'We'll both of us be ruined if they find out what we've done today.'*

He'd held the bottle out to her and she'd scrambled up to sit beside him, taken it from his hands and put it to her own lips. Together they had drunk that bottle dry.

Whilst Tombar was enjoying a slice of cake and a glass of fresh goat's milk in what had once been Jake and Kath Allen's farm cottage, Annabelle lay back on her bed, reliving the day that she had confided in her uncle, telling him that she would soon be giving birth to Jake Allen's child. She hadn't ever considered confiding in either Charlotte or Rebecka. She'd been praying that her cousins would never know of the shameful thing that she had done. The Trelawny family, a great and well respected family, had taken her to their hearts and given her nothing but love and respect over the last twelve years. How could she repay that love by presenting them with an illegitimate child; a child who would be whispered about throughout the land; a child who would not exist but for her own selfishness and stupidity. She had never for a moment blamed Jake. She had pursued him relentlessly; walked uninvited into his house when she had known that, for some reason, he was vulnerable and that he would be there alone. Her uncle though had not agreed with her. She had been sure that he would know what to do, sure that if anyone could help her it would be Sir Jonathan Trelawny, a man who had not been afraid to put his God before his King and risk his life because of it.

She had told him the truth and he had listened, as she had known he would, but he had not seemed to understand that she had been entirely to blame.
'You acted very foolishly, Annabelle,' he'd said. *'But this man took advantage of your foolishness and of your compassion for him. For this he will have to pay a high price. Jake Allen and his wife will have to leave my estate. It is clear that you are already suffering and I can only do my best to ease that for you. I cannot end it, Annabelle. I have connections and can arrange for you to go away to have your child. We will tell everyone that you are visiting with relations on your mother's side of the family. This should not arouse suspicion since we are all used to you spending a few weeks with one relative or another throughout the spring or early summer. You*

will have to return here as soon as possible after the birth and I will see to it that the Allens are no longer living at Trelawne when you return. A good home will be found for the child, Annabelle. You need have no concerns over the welfare of your baby.'

'A child should be raised by its own flesh and blood uncle,' she'd said. *'If it is possible it should be raised within its own family.'*
He'd been shocked by her words.
'I understood from our conversation that you wanted nothing to do with this baby, Annabelle. Did you not express the wish that no one in the family should be embarrassed by your indiscretion? Are you telling me now that you want to keep it?'
'No.' she'd said. *'But my baby has a father whose dearest wish is to have children. I have had a long time to think about all of this uncle. I do not want to keep the baby myself, but I want you to ask Jake Allen and his wife if they want this child. I want it raised by its own father.'*

He had lapsed into a long silence but then shocked her by laughing.
'I do believe, Annabelle, that you are more like me than any of my own children. This whole affair will have to be given much thought and be handled very carefully. It will indeed be a miracle if we are to achieve all of this and never be discovered.'

It seemed though that they had been granted that small miracle. Her uncle had sent for Jake in the evening of the very day that she had confided in him. She had never known what really passed between them behind the closed doors of the library, but she had been told of the outcome.

The Trelawny family had owned land and a long abandoned old farmhouse on a desolate part of Bodmin Moor. Only Jake Allen had known why he'd been sent out onto that moorland to live in that farmhouse and bring it back to life; to work on that land until it yielded crops that he had harvested and stored, to feed the animals that were housed in barns that he had built with his own hands. Only he had known that the child who had been given to them was his own child, and that his wife was never to learn that the boy was her own husband's son, or that his mother was Annabelle Trelawny.

Her uncle had visited the couple in their farm cottage at Trelawne to speak with Kath Allen.

'I want my land out on Bodmin Moor turned back into a working farm,' he'd said. *'I want the old house occupied again before it falls apart from neglect.'*

He had been told, he'd said, by members of his family, that she was a good Christian, a regular churchgoer in nearby Looe, along with her sister and her sister's small children.

'I believe that your husband is the right man to carry out this task for me,' he'd said, *'but I am concerned that you will no longer be able to walk to*

your sister's house and spend time with your nieces and nephews, or indeed to attend church with them. There are churches on the moor at St Breward, Blisland, Temple and of course the most splendid is at Altarnun, our cathedral on the moor. They are all though between four and five miles away from the farm where you are to live, and the land that you will have to cross is uninhabited and dangerous. It is not safe for a woman on her own to try to cross that moor.'

'This will not keep me from going to church, Sir,' she'd replied. *'Jake will take me across the moor. He has not been inside a church since our boy died five years back, but we have the horse and cart and he will take me. I am grateful though for your concern. It is true that I will miss my sister's children as we have none of our own. We both want another baby, but our prayers are not being answered.'*

He had told her that it saddened him as the father of a large family himself, to meet others who were in desperate need of a child, when he knew of many babies born to unfortunate young women, who could not take those children home to their families.

'We do what we can my dear,' he'd said. *'The church does what it can for these little ones, but it is not easy to find someone who will bring them up as their own.'*

It had been Kath Allen who had asked if she could be given one of these babies. Kath who had said that they would love it, that the old farmhouse would be a home with a child there to care for. And Jake had agreed.

The Allen's had been sent to live out on Bodmin Moor, and she had been sent to Winchester to be cared for and delivered of her baby boy in a large and comfortable household where several Protestant ladies had formed a little community caring for young women of gentle birth, who had, like herself, fallen by the wayside. Her real identity had not ever been revealed, even to those saintly ladies, and her child had been taken from her almost as soon as he'd drawn his first breath.

She had given Jake a son, and later sought solace for herself in the gift that he had unwittingly given to her; the comfort that could be found in a bottle of gin.

Chapter Three

Summer of 1749

The tide was out, as he had known it would be, and a vast expanse of golden sand stretched out, almost as far away as he could see in that bright sunlight towards the shimmering waters of the English Channel. Reining in his quivering horse he dismounted, shaking off his rough shirt to let the sun's rays burn into his skin. The horse shifted restlessly beside him, eager to go; eager to race across the soft sand to the water's edge and trot through the foamy waves for a while to cool her legs.

"Not today my beauty," he murmured, "not in this heat. I'll walk you to the cave and we can rest awhile in the shade."

It had been the hottest summer that he could remember, in all of his tender fifteen years, and crossing the moor that day had been hard on them both. He'd taken the shortest route, using the secluded pathways that he'd found on his frequent journeys to Looe and to the coast; well-trodden pathways that he knew were only used at night as he'd never once met another living soul when he'd travelled along them in daylight. He'd heard tales of smuggling; goods plundered from shipwrecks and hidden in caves along the shoreline, to be picked up in the dead of night and trekked silently across the moor to some secret destination. These were paths used by smugglers, he was certain of that, and he'd come to the beach today to return to a cave that he'd stumbled across on his last visit there. There had been no time to explore on that occasion, but he'd found the smouldering remains of a little fire on a natural stone ledge, quite close inside the entrance. Someone had been there not long before him.

Removing his shoes to walk his horse slowly across the loose, warm sand, he quickly slipped them on again as they reached the shadows of dark ancient cliffs. Rough shingle replaced soft sand and beyond the shingle there were rocks and little pools hidden by slippery seaweed. The air was cold here beneath the overhanging rocks, but welcome after the relentless heat of the sun. His horse, usually so sure footed, was treading carefully, testing the ground beneath her at each step forward, and slowing their progress. Patiently he stayed beside her, his eyes constantly searching the cliff, watching for the dark hole in the rock face, the opening that was the entrance to that well concealed cave.

He saw the smoke first and then a red glow at the base of the cliffside. He had found the cave again but this time someone had lit a small fire on the rocks, just to one side of the entrance. He was about to turn and walk away; save his skin; leave the

murderous smugglers alone to gloat over their ill-gotten gains, when he realised that it was too late. A young black man, no older than himself, had come out from the darkness of that gaping hole in the cliff and was already walking towards him. His heartbeat quickened at the sight of the long handled fire fork, held up high in the youth's hand and the large fish impaled upon it. But then, and with a sudden sharp intake of breath, he realised that this was no smuggler.
"Tombar?" he said as they drew close to each other. "Tell me that you are not about to kill me with that fire fork. Tell me that I am right, and that you are Tombar from the Trelawny estate."
"Tell me who is asking," came his reply, but it was said with a smile as the fork was lowered and held between them.
"I'm Jon Allen from Hele Farm, out on Bodmin Moor. I was named for Sir Jonathan, the Trelawny who gave us the farmhouse and the land out there. So, you are Tombar?"
"You can rest easy, Jon Allen. I am Tombar from Trelawne. I don't know how you know my name, but come over to the fire and tell me about yourself. Share my fish with me if you are hungry. I caught them this morning when the tide was in. I have plenty more inside the cave."

They sat on the rocks together, swallowing mouthful after mouthful of freshly cooked fish and talking with the ease of old friends.
"Has no-one ever told you that you are close to a legend in this part of Cornwall, Tombar? I remember

being told, about seven years back, that an African boy was living at the manor house. My grandmother said that you had run away from slavery to come to Cornwall with Annabelle Trelawny. My grandparents lived at Trelawne when they were first married, farmed the land that was closest to the estate. She told me everything about the Trelawnys. And when you came, she told me about Jamaica; about the slave ships and the sugar plantations. I want to go there one day. I want to travel; see the world. The furthest I've ever been away from home is when we go to towns nearby on market days, or come here to Looe to visit with my great aunt and her family."

"But you'll be able to go away one day, surely, when you're older. What's to stop you?"

"The farm. It will be mine one day. My father had no brothers or sisters and I am his only child. My mother died when I was born."

"What happened to your grandfather?"

"My grandmother always says that he died from sheer hard work. They were sent out to live on land that hadn't been farmed in years. Sir Jonathan wanted it turned back into a working farm and my grandfather did that for him; all on his own. Grandma Kath says it killed him in the end. When he died though, Sir Jonathan gave the house and the land to my father. Said he had no more use for it himself and that my grandfather had paid for it, with the sweat of his brow."

"So you are wealthy now then are you? You and your father and your grandma Kath?"

Jon laughed. “Not exactly wealthy, Tombar. But we’ve prospered. Done well enough to take on hired help and live a good life. I have my own horse and enough free time to roam around on the moors and on this beach. My grandfather did well for us though he never lived to see it.”

“Would you like to see the farm where he started out, Jon? Take me back to Trelawne now on your horse and I’ll take you to the cottage where he used to live.”

“I’m afraid that I’ll wake up and find that I’ve been dreaming all of this! I came here to explore a cave and instead I’m going to Trelawne with Tombar, the stowaway from Jamaica!”

“Well there’s nothing much to see in the cave my friend. The only thing I’ve ever found in there is this.” He tugged at the chain that was around his neck, pulling a large pendant out from inside his shirt. “I wear it when I go fishing,” he said as he took it off to give to Jon. “It always brings me luck. Here, what do you make of it?”

“It’s heavy,” Jon said as he turned it over in his hand. “What kind of stone changes colour like this? It’s changing as I tilt it.”

“I wouldn’t know, but I think the metal must be silver. It’s just badly discoloured with age.”

“Why don’t you try to clean it up? Bring it with us now and we’ll see what we can do for it with some silver polish. It may have some value. Could be hidden treasure from a shipwreck!”

“I don’t feel that it’s mine to take. Come and see where I keep it. I was climbing about in the cave one day. Thought I saw a bat, and I found this pendant quite high up, lying on a small ledge. When I leave, I always put it back. It belongs here for now, but someone will come for it one day."

It was less than two miles to Trelawne and they had journeyed in silence, each lost in his own thoughts until they were close by to the manor house, and Jon stopped his horse on the edge of a grassy slope that led down to the gardens at the front of the Trelawny's ancestral home. Someone had lit a small bonfire at one side of the manor, not far from the turreted clock tower, but the fire had travelled, to trickle along a line of debris that had been swept against the old house, and creep up through the dry stems of ivy that clung to the outer walls and around the partly open ground floor windows.

Jon leapt off his horse and Tombar followed.
"We'll leave my horse here where it is safe. Come on. There's no one else around. I don't think anyone's noticed!"
Jon ran ahead of Tombar, who had stopped for a second, to watch in horror as the drapes inside the dining room windows were suddenly engulfed in flames.
"Where's your well, Tombar?" Jon was looking anxiously around as Tombar joined him.
"In the courtyard at the back."
"Well, rouse the servants! Alert the whole household. Send them to the well with buckets, anything. Tell them to form a line inside the house to pass water along from the well to that room. The fire's caught the furniture, so they must act quickly.

Bring me any containers you can lay your hands on. We can stop the fire from spreading out here with water from the pond!"
As Tombar ran off into the manor, Jon swiftly kicked all of the unlit debris away from the trickling line of fire that would have spread around the two low steps that were outside of the main entrance. As the flames crawled upwards to surround a second open window, he jumped up, to stand on the sill, desperately trying to reach the little casement windows that were open at the top and save the room inside from destruction. But their handles were out of reach and he was forced to drop to the ground as the fire caught at his trouser leg. Running to drench his leg with water from the pond, he saw that Tombar was there before him, filling pots and pans gathered up from the kitchen with the precious water. The first panful extinguished the flame around Jon's leg and then their fight began to put out the fire around the second window.

"We're losing this, Jon. We need help out here." Tombar groaned as the fire began to spread, travelling up through the clinging stems of ivy and out of their reach. And, as if in answer to a prayer, help arrived. Reg Clemo came around from the farthest wing of the house, beside the Bishop's Chapel, accompanied by his small son and two young wagoners, all guiding something between them, something bulky, something on wheels.
"A fire cart! Praise be, they've brought a fire cart!" Jon ran to help them guide the old water pump over to the main site of the fire.

"We've filled the trough," Reg said, "but we'll need you both to help work the pump handles. I'll direct the water pipe."

More help arrived as people came from all directions, carrying water from the well to refill the trough at the centre of the cart, and as the young wagoners took charge of the two long pump handles at the front end, Tombar and Jon worked the handles at the rear. The flames around the windows were the first to be extinguished, and before long the water directed from the pipe, was quenching the fire on the front of the house.

Two women walked slowly together to empty the last of their water laden buckets, and afterwards moved back, exhausted and bedraggled, to stand beside Tombar and Jon, who were still working tirelessly on the pumps.

"It's over, Charlotte," Annabelle said. "We've beaten it in the dining room and it's almost over out here."

Jon overheard her. "It could still smoulder and catch up again," he said. "Someone should be inside to watch it."

Exchanging a quick glance the two women hurried off towards the main entrance. He called out after them. "Make sure you close up all the windows!"

Tombar smiled as the women increased their speed and Annabelle held up her hand without even a glance behind her.

"You'll have to watch yourself," he said, "ordering the ladies of the house around like that."
Jon was frowning. "But they looked as tired and wet through as the rest of us. Have they been standing alongside their servants, fighting the fire in the dining room?"
"Why wouldn't they Jon? Trelawne is their home."

The fire was out. Jon wandered over to speak to Reg Clemo and Tombar slipped away to search for Charlotte or Annabelle. He found them together in the doorway to the dining room, looking in at the charred remains of their furniture. Part of the ceiling had collapsed and the damage to the room was extensive.
"Tombar!" Charlotte greeted him warmly as he appeared behind them. "I believe that we have you to thank for saving the house from far more damage than we see here before us. The servants are saying that if it weren't for your actions today, many more rooms may have suffered the same fate as this one."
Suspecting that Jon may insist on returning to his home that evening; riding injured and alone across Bodmin Moor in failing light, Tombar quickly explained the events of the day to the incredulous women, and ran back outside to speak to his new friend.
"Miss Charlotte is saying that you must stay here at the manor tonight," he told Jon, "she is sending for a doctor to come out from Looe and tend to the burn on your leg."
"I should leave, Tombar. My family will worry if I don't get back by nightfall."

"I've told them all about your family, and Miss Annabelle has promised to send a wagoner out to your farm at first light, to tell them that you are safe. She came over quite faint poor soul, just as I was saying that your family owned the old Trelawny farm out on Bodmin Moor, and that your grandparents once farmed land here at Trelawne. She has gone upstairs to rest now but they both want to meet you in the morning Jon. I am to take you to meet them in the Great Hall tomorrow morning at eleven o'clock."

A comfortable, makeshift bed was made up for Jon on the floor of Tombar's room that night, but as one of them was in great pain, and the other was more than willing to stay awake, they settled down, not to sleep, but to talk the night away.

Jon's trusty horse had been cared for in the stables overnight and both young men paid her a visit in the morning, well before they were expected in the Great Hall. Satisfied that she was in no distress, they wandered over to see what damage had been done to the front of the house.

"Not too much harm suffered out here. I should think a good clean and a little restoration will be all that is needed," Jon said, pulling a little of the blackened ivy away from the stonework.

"Houses don't suffer like people, Jon. Your leg will need more than a little restoration before it ceases to give you pain"

Annabelle Trelawny was sitting alone on the settle in the Great Hall to greet Tombar and Jon as they came in from the gardens that morning.

"I am sorry Jon," she said, "but my cousin is not well enough to come downstairs today. I fear that she may have been awake throughout the entire night, worrying over the damage to the dining room. Trelawne is her brother Edward's house you see and, as he is in Jamaica, he will not know anything of this for many weeks. She has asked me to thank you though Jon, for everything that you did for us yesterday. Tombar has said that he was under your instructions when he told our servants to form the line that enabled them to deliver water so quickly to the dining room. And you have been injured. We owe you a great deal young man."
"It was your fire cart that ended it though…… Miss ….. We couldn't stop the fire outside the house."
He didn't know what to call her. Her own grandson didn't know what to call her.

There was no doubt in her mind that this boy was her son's child. One look at his pale, untidy hair and wide grey eyes had been all that she'd needed to be sure of that.
"Edward had that fire cart brought here," she said, "not long before we set sail for Jamaica. I think that we had all forgotten it, except for Reg Clemo that is. He knew that it had been put away years ago, out in the old stable block and, thank the Lord, it saved the house. But you gained us valuable time Jon. Your quick thinking gave us the time that it took for Reg

to get to the house, pull out the old fire cart, and fill it with water from the well. I really don't know where we would be if Tombar hadn't brought you here to us yesterday. There must be something we can do for you in return."

"Nothing." Jon shook his head. "I don't want anything … except." He was looking around the room. "I'm sorry, Miss. Could I sit down? My leg ….."

"Of course. I'm not thinking. You must be in pain. Sit beside me here on the settle. And you Tombar. Come and sit beside Jon." She moved a little way along the settle so that they could sit together.

"Is that all that you want then young man? Just to sit down?"

He smiled, a generous smile, so much like her own, and just for a moment she saw Jake in his eyes; drowsy, amused eyes, so much like his grandfather's.

"We were talking last night, Miss, in fact we were talking for most of the night, about the years Tombar spent in Jamaica and what it's like for him now, living here at Trelawne, and for my family, living out on the moor. I told him about the inn, the coaching house that's to be built on a part of our land next year and the road that is to follow, but it's best that Tombar talks to you about this. He knows what I want to ask of you."

"Jon wants to ask you if I can help to build the inn, Miss Annabelle. He wants me to live out on his family's farm for a while next year, and work with him to help build Jamaica Inn."

"Jamaica Inn! A coaching house out in the middle of Bodmin Moor and a road built across wasteland! Such a road would surely take years to build, and what use will there be for a coaching house if there are no proper roads?"

"The road has already been started, Miss." Jon answered her. "My father says there is a need for a road through the centre of the county, a route over the moor for the mail riders and the stage wagons. A proper road will run between Launceston and Bodmin one day. But before it is a proper road the old packhorse ways will be levelled and made wide enough for coaches to use. My father's been saying that load after load of stone and rubble will be thrown into the ruts already made by carts and horses. He says the coaches will soon grind them in."

Tombar interrupted him. "There will be stables built where the drivers can change horses, and rooms in the inn, where travellers could stay overnight if they wish to."

"Well I knew nothing of this until now. I have been living away from Cornwall for most of the year Jon, staying with a friend in Surrey. I only returned to Trelawne three days ago. But can you tell me why this coaching house is to be known as Jamaica Inn?"

It was Tombar who answered her. "Jon says it's in honour of Mr Edward, as he's the Governor of Jamaica."

"Well I'm sure that my cousin will approve. And you don't need my permission if this is what you want to do, Tombar. You are not a servant here. This is your home and, although you have chosen to work here, you can leave Trelawne whenever you wish. I thought you knew that."

Tombar nodded. "I do want to help build the inn with Jon next year, but I can't leave Trelawne. I can't leave my home. I have to be here when you come back to us, Miss Annabelle."

"But you can always return to Trelawne, Tombar. Your room will still be here for you, and there will be work for you to do, if that is what you wish. As for me, well I may not be returning to Cornwall quite so often my dear. I have some news that I haven't yet shared with anyone, not even with Charlotte. I am to be married next year Tombar. I have finally met someone who is very dear to me, and he has asked me to be his wife."

"Married Miss Annabelle! But you have never been married."

"Please don't be concerned for me, Tombar," Annabelle laughed, "I am very happy and my future husband is a good man. You can be sure that he will look after me. He has already said that you will always be welcome in his house. He lives in Surrey, quite a long way from here, but you must come up for our wedding next year. You must both come up for our wedding! That is, of course, if you will be able to tear yourselves away from helping to build your Jamaica Inn."

Chapter Four

Autumn of 1777

An ominous black cloud hung over much of the landscape as Tombar strode out across the three fields that lay between Hele Farm and Jamaica Inn. The thunderous blot on the horizon totally obscured any sign of the early morning sun, seeming to rise from the land beneath the coaching house and envelope it, taunting him, hiding it from him.

His love for the coaching house that he had helped to build had kept him out on the moor for almost thirty years, living at Hele Farm with Jon's family, but working for the most part at the inn. He'd had little time for himself, as the drivers of post chaises, long wagons and stage coaches had stopped by the stables to change horses, whilst their weary passengers rested, or even stayed for a night inside the house. The new turnpike road between Launceston and Bodmin had breathed life into the inn and she had flourished, but the travellers who still used the old roads, the well-trodden pathways that led from the coast across cliff tops and moorland, had also forged new tracks for themselves, tracks that twisted between steep banks and across tortuous hilly ground, bringing villains and smugglers alike, directly to Jamaica Inn.

As he reached the yard outside of the stables he was surprised to see a long wagon, with eight horses, standing out front of the main entrance to the inn. There were no passengers to be found inside the clumsy covered wagon, just parcels and packages, and since there seemed to be no driver around outside of the house, Tombar made his way into the inn and towards the tempting smell of bacon, frying over the peat fire in the kitchen. Ginny Rodda, the innkeeper's wife, was busy preparing a meal for four strangers, one young man, two middle aged women and a boy, who were all seated around the well-scrubbed table in the middle of the room. Only Ginny looked at him as he entered the kitchen, her face flushed and accusing.

"And where were you may I ask, when the mail arrived in the night? I was roused from my warm bed to help the chaise driver change his horses. The poor man was expecting your help, Tom! I bore the brunt of his curses when that wild mare of yours knocked him to the stable floor!"

"Where was that husband of yours then, Ginny? He was the one who told me to stay in my bed last night, and I wasn't going to argue with him over it. He could manage the mail and I was to stay out of the way. Those were his words when I left here at nightfall. You'd best take it up with him."

Since she didn't reply he turned to walk away but the man at the table turned anxiously to look at him.
"I'll need some help to change two of my team," he said, "but I'm not good myself around horses that don't know me."
Tombar nodded at him. "I'll be outside," he said.

"Tom." Ginny glanced up at him as she brought bread and dripping to the table for her guests. "There'll be bacon on the plate for you if you care to come back a bit later."
The anger had gone from her voice now, but Tombar's heart was heavy as he walked towards the stable. The London Inn, just five miles down on the road, was the last pull off for a change of horses before Bodmin. The innkeeper there was old Bill Couch, and he would be cursing if the mail driver had taken Wild Nell for his team in the night. She was only content in her own stable when darkness fell, and had been known to near kick the stalls down at the London, and the King's Head at Five Lanes, if they'd not sent her back to Jamaica before nightfall.

He whistled softly as he crossed the yard and she answered him with a loud whinny that straightaway lifted his low spirits. She wasn't his horse, as Ginny had just suggested, but he didn't fear her as most others did. She'd been unpredictable from the start; more than five years had gone by since she'd first been brought to the inn, but he'd worked with her and gained her trust where others had failed, so that now she was known as his horse, and he was given most of the handling of her.

After selecting two of the most rested horses in the stable to help pull the long wagon to the London Inn, Tombar stood in the yard for a while to await the return of its driver and passengers. Their journey would be slow and uncomfortable, but obtaining a seat in one of these goods wagons was a cheap way to travel and a sure one, as their wide wheels made easy work of the muddy potholed roads.

The cloud had lifted now and he could see across the fields to Hele Farm and beyond, through the passageway between the cow byre and the inn. But this was all to change in the New Year when the Jamaica Inn and the surrounding area were to be greatly altered. The old passageway through to the back of the house would be lost then, as the building was to be widened and a new stable block and tack room were to be built onto the front of the cow byre, joining up with the inn. The granite stone work of the newly enlarged coaching house was all to be covered in slate to cloak the alterations.

Until now Jamaica Inn had stood proudly on the hill beneath Tolborough Tor with only Hele Farm for company, but, at the same time as the inn was to be altered, a handful of small cottages were to be built on the far side of the road. Jamaica Inn had brought changes to what was only a small part of Bodmin Moor, and now she was to be changed herself, but it was the recent alterations to Tombar's own life that were the cause of his low spirits, and he could see no easy way around them.

For almost twenty years the Allen's farmhouse had housed only Jon's father William, Jon, Tombar and two or sometimes three farm workers. No women had slept beneath its ancient roof since Kath Allen had passed away in the winter of 1759. Consequently Mary Allen had found the old place to be sorely in need of a woman's touch when she came to Hele Farm as Jon's bride in the spring of 1776. The sweet natured farmer's daughter from Halworthy had wasted little time in turning what had become no more than a bare and dreary dwelling house, into a cheery and far more comfortable place to live.

After the death of her father, Mary had inherited Gilbert Farm, where she had been brought up as the only surviving child of David and Elizabeth Hocken. Her two older brothers had both passed away before reaching their seventh birthdays, and as Henry, the youngest of them had been born only fourteen months before Mary, and died at the tender age of five years and a few days, she had grown up from the age of three years as an only, and much doted on child.

Her father had managed his farm with the help of a small team of men who lived close by in the village of Halworthy, and Mary had led a sheltered life, watched over constantly by her mother who had taught her treasured daughter how to cook and to sew as well as how to read and to write, but had kept her on the farm, out of harms' way, and as much as possible, away from the company of others.

Mary had been in her early twenties when Elizabeth Hocken had died suddenly one night in her sleep, and less than a year later, after a long and debilitating illness, her father had followed his wife to her grave. Mary's secluded upbringing had left her unable to cope alone with the day to day running of the farm, and she was quickly persuaded to sell the house, the land and her possessions and start a new life for herself somewhere close by; somewhere where she could buy a little cottage and live for a while as a woman of independent means.

One chilly but sunny day in the autumn of 1775, Mary had taken her pony and trap into Halworthy to look at a cottage that had only recently been vacated and was now available for potential buyers to view. Stabling her pony behind the local inn, she had soon discovered that she had not chosen a good day to come to Halworthy in search of a particular cottage. It was market day and the crowded, noisy little streets were further narrowed by the many market stalls, and the men, women and children who were gathered around them. Mary was looking for Bellringer's Cottage and was carefully picking her way through the people, hoping to find the attractively named cottage, when she'd noticed a man walking slowly towards her, a tall, broad shouldered black man who was laughing and talking, to the equally tall and fair haired man at his side. Mary hadn't ever seen a black person before, man, woman or child, and so she'd stared at him, fascinated, unable to tear her eyes away from his smiling face and completely unaware that the man by his side had noticed her and was watching, highly amused as the pretty well-rounded young woman with beautiful brown eyes had drawn gradually closer; breathtakingly beautiful eyes that were fixed on his friend. As she'd reached them he'd stepped straight out in front of her, so that she'd walked into his open arms, and for a moment or two he'd held onto her, apologising for not paying attention to where he'd been walking. She'd been embarrassed; moving back a little as he'd released her, apologising herself for not having paid any attention to where she'd been going; explaining that she was a stranger to the village and looking for Bellringer's Cottage.

"As it happens," he'd said, "I know the cottage well, but it is quite hidden away in one of the back streets. I would be happy to take you there, but first let me introduce myself. I am Jon Allen and this is my good friend Tombar. We live on my father's farm close to Jamaica Inn on Bodmin Moor."
"I am Mary Hocken," she'd replied, "and I am hoping to buy Bellringers Cottage, but I am sure that I can find it on my own, if you'd just point me in the right direction."
"Nonsense," he'd said, "I will take you there, unless of course you would prefer it if Tom showed you the way?"

She had smiled at Tom, but linked her arm through Jon's, grateful for his company and shyly aware of her attraction to his sleepy grey eyes and untidy fair hair.

Bellringer's Cottage, with its musty, cramped rooms had not appealed to Mary, but as she and Jon had almost instantly fallen in love with each other, she had no longer needed to search for a cottage where she could live on her own. Instead she had accepted Jon's proposal of marriage and had become Mrs Jon Allen in the following year, at the end of March. They had both desperately wanted children, and so it came as no surprise to William Allen or to Tom when, in the early summer of 1777, Jon had announced that Mary was expecting his child. For a while it had seemed that the couple were even happier than before, but sadly this was to change suddenly one particularly warm afternoon at the end of July, when Mary had accompanied her husband and father-in-law on their monthly visit to Halworthy market. She had wanted to look at the stalls, buy things for the house and for the baby, and so the men had left her to browse on her own, while they went into the inn for a drink before paying a visit to the livestock auction to look over the stock.

In the short time that she had known Jon, Mary had grown to love the bustle of market days, the conversations shared with people who recognised her now as Jon Allen's wife, or William Allen's daughter-in-law. She was fast becoming a part of the little community to which she had really belonged for the whole of her life, but where no-one recognised her as Mary Hocken who had lived out on Gilbert Farm, less than a mile from the village of Halworthy. Her mother had taught her to knit and to sew, and she had come to the market today to look for suitable material with which she could make her own baby's clothes. She was also hoping to get into conversation with at least one young mother, and glean some information that would help her to care for the infant that she hoped to soon hold in her arms, for her mother had certainly taught her nothing at all about newborn babies.

Amongst the last few stalls in the street that day, she'd noticed one that she was sure she'd not seen before. An elderly lady was sitting on an equally elderly chair, smiling out at everyone who passed her by, from behind tall piles of very small sheets and blankets, and an array of tiny white baby clothes.

"Have you made all of these yourself?" Mary asked as she turned over the little nightdresses and jackets.

"I've been making them for months now my dear, hoping to make a little money for myself to put food on the table." The old lady had sighed as she'd peered up at Mary. "Most women make their own so they tell me, or their babies wear the clothes handed down from other little ones as they've grown away. I've not had many interested in my efforts so far today."

"Oh, but I am interested." Mary had picked up a little knitted hat and some mittens. "God willing, my baby will be born in the winter, and I do plan to make its little clothes, but although I can make dresses for myself, and curtains for the windows, I have never made anything as small as these lovely little garments. I will buy one of everything that you have here for my baby to wear, and I will also be able to use them as patterns for the clothes that I make."

"God bless you my dear," the old lady had said as Mary had gathered up the garments and paid for all of her purchases.

"I saw a young woman selling pasties from a stall, just a few minutes ago. She has a tiny baby with her. I will show her these clothes and hope that she comes to buy something from you. Do you think that she will let me hold her child? I know nothing at all about such small children you see. My husband says that I will know what to do when our baby is born, but I am not so sure. My mother has passed away you see, and I have no sisters or sisters-in-law to turn to."

The old lady was looking quite concerned. "Forgive me," she'd said, "but are you a stranger to these parts? Are you saying that you don't know a living soul around here who has cared for a baby?"

"I was born on Gilbert Farm, not a mile from here, but I was kept on the farm with only my parents for company for most of my life. Soon after my father died, I met the man who became my husband. We live out on Bodmin Moor, on Hele Farm with my father-in-law, and our only neighbours are the innkeeper and his wife from Jamaica Inn. I have not met either of them, but they have no children."

"Oh my dear, I knew your family! I met them for the first time right here in the village when you were just a very small girl, hopping around their feet, so full of energy, and your poor mother and father having to carry your older brothers everywhere they went. Poor little cripples, dying so young as well. Your mother explained to me that her own brothers had suffered the self-same affliction. I told her that she was lucky to have you, but after her boys had all passed away, we never saw her again in the village, or you for that matter. You must be so worried. I will pray for you my dear. I will pray for your baby and ask that your family's misfortune will pass you by."

Mary had seemed inconsolable. She had known that she'd had brothers; the youngest of them had been little more than a year older than herself and that they had both passed away before her own fourth birthday. Her parents had rarely spoken of their sons, and as time had gone by, her mother had swiftly changed the subject whenever Mary had mentioned her brothers. She had only one memory she'd said. A vivid memory of a little boy with a heart-warming smile and eyes as black as coal, being carried high in her father's arms. She had never been told that her brothers were unable to walk; never realised that they had been crippled.

Haunted by the old woman's words, *"I will pray that your family's misfortune will pass you by,"* poor

Mary had seemed convinced that her own baby would suffer the same affliction as her brothers and uncles.

As the summer had faded into autumn, so Mary had faded with it. The warmth had gone from her smile, and her face had paled and become thinner with each passing day. Gradually the heart had gone out of her, and now, as autumn had finally turned to winter, William Allen and Tom saw little of her, as she mostly took to her bed whilst they were in the house, and although Jon now prepared all of their food and took Mary's meals to her, he often returned to the kitchen with very little gone from the plate.

Before Tom had left the farm that morning, he'd found Jon alone in the kitchen and told him that he was planning to move out of the farmhouse.

"I've been thinking that maybe we are too close Jon, you and I," he'd said. "Maybe Mary would be happier if I weren't here with you every day. I don't exactly pull my weight around the farm either as I'm working up at the inn, but she still has to wash my clothes and clean up after me. It may be easier for her with me out of the way."
But Jon would have none of it. "Mary's heartache is over our child, Tom. It has nothing to do with your living here with us, and you know it!" He'd brought a pot of tea to the table. "The baby will be born soon, and my father says that Mary will see everything differently then. He says that she will love it from the moment that she sets eyes on it, and

to her it will be perfect, however things turn out. Besides, if it weren't for you working up there at the inn and helping those scoundrels to hide their tubs and packages away from the customs, we wouldn't be sharing your rewards. Mary's been more than happy with the silk and the lace that you've brought her, and we'd be paying high taxes on this tea, and the ale that fills our bellies every night! You're not leaving us Tom. I won't hear of it! Unless of course you have a woman of your own to go to. Is that it Tom? Do you have a woman somewhere that you've kept hidden from me?"

Unwittingly Jon had touched on the other cause of Tom's low spirits, for he did have a woman to go to, but not one of his own.

Charles Davey and his wife Emma had kept the inn for the previous six years, right up until the summer just gone, but their only daughter had been a sickly child and they had thought it best to move off the moor and live in a town where there were doctors close by to call on. Charles had found work in one of Bodmin's many taverns, and Jim Rodda from nearby Halworthy had replaced him as the new innkeeper on the moor. Through the years the inn had seen both landlords and innkeepers come and go. Some had stayed for years and some for just a few months, but mostly they had got on well enough with Tombar. They had needed him out there on that lonely and inhospitable moorland for he knew everything that there was to know about Jamaica Inn. He'd helped to build her granite walls and had grown to love the house which had proudly housed so many weary travellers over time. Beneath her slate roof they had slept, filled their bellies, slaked their thirst, and warmed their bones beside her smouldering peat fires; fires that seemed to leap a little higher whenever he or Jon warmed themselves beside them.

"She knows her boys," Emma Davey had said one evening to a small group of people just in off the stage coach. They had all turned to watch the flames leap up into the chimney as Tombar and Jon had joined them all in the bar, and moved across to stand beside the fireplace.

"Those two helped to build this place when they were little more than children, and they've lived and worked around here ever since. Greets them like a mother greets her sons she does!"

"To the sons of Jamaica Inn then," one friendly old man had said, raising his glass to Tombar and Jon. "I've always said that every building has a soul, and you've confirmed it for me gentlemen. God bless you!"

Jim Rodda had been no different to his predecessors, amicable enough; paying Tombar to work on the farm or help out in the stables, and more than grateful for his presence when they'd had goods dropped off or picked up in the dead of night. The smugglers who came to the inn with their hastily blackened faces, their bodies padded out with parcels and their packhorses laden down with barrels, were mostly local men. Over time they had come to know and trust Tombar, but they were often suspicious of new innkeepers and their families. Tombar's presence had been a great comfort for Jim Rodda, and indeed for his young wife Ginny. But Ginny had found Tombar's presence a little more than a comfort. She had taken a shine to him from the start, and to his embarrassment had done little to hide it from Jim. She had openly flirted and teased and spent time in his company which, in his opinion, she should have been spending with her husband. To Tombar's amazement Jim seemed to make nothing of it, and so he'd felt safe enough to bring the subject up when they were sat together one night in the kitchen, waiting for the mail coach to arrive. But Jim had just laughed.

"Don't worry yourself Tom," he'd said. "I know you've not encouraged her. She's taken a fancy to you right enough and who can blame her. Lord knows I don't pay her much attention, but she knew what to expect when she married me. Likely she'll tell you about it if you ask her. But I'll have a word with her in the morning and tell her you're tired of her teasing and carryings-on. How does that please you?"

Tom had nodded, but he'd known even then that it was too late. Ginny had recently told him that Jim had no interest in her, and that he had a mistress in Halworthy. Tom's embarrassment had already turned into amusement and affection, and over the following three months this affection had developed into feelings so deep and so strong that he couldn't take his eyes off her when they were together, and he now wanted to be together with her for the rest of his life. Only two mornings ago he'd put his arms around her waist and pressed a kiss on the back of her neck as she'd stood at the kitchen table with her back towards him. She'd turned to him, tilting her face upwards for his kisses and had only pulled away at the sound of footsteps in the passageway outside the door. It had been Jim, looking for his breakfast, and Tom had left them, making some excuse to go outside. He hadn't been alone with her since then.

After watching the long wagon trundle slowly out of the yard and back onto the road, Tom hastily stabled the two tired mares that had been up front of its eight horse team, and returned to Ginny in the kitchen.
"Jim's horse is gone from its stall. Did he leave you alone here in the night?"
"I wouldn't have been out of my bed wrestling with that horse of yours if Jim had been here. He rode off soon after you'd gone down to the farm. Said he'd be back in the early hours to see to the mail, and that he'd be waiting up afterwards for a delivery."
"A delivery? But he told me to stay out of the way. He must have known they wouldn't be here in the night or he'd have come back."
"Someone did come by, Tom, but it was just a man with a horse and cart. He left a sack full of potatoes out in the back room and told me not to touch them. They are to be picked up just before nightfall."

Tom disappeared through the little door in the corner of the kitchen which led into a store room for provisions. He soon returned, dragging a heavy sack out into the middle of the floor.
"You can be sure there's more than potatoes in that sack, Ginny. And I'll wager it's something a bit different to tea or tobacco. Something he didn't want me to know about. I'll take a look at them while I'm waiting for that bacon you promised me earlier."

"If you've got the time to search through a sack of old potatoes," she said, crossing the room to wrap her arms around his neck, "then you've got the time to make love to me."
He kissed her, holding her face in his hands.
"Have you got no shame Ginny Rodda? Your husband could be riding back to you as we speak."
"Jim don't want me Tom. I've told you before. He married me but he's got a woman in Halworthy. That's where he went last night."
That's as maybe, but you're still his wife. I wouldn't want him catching us together."
He stroked her hair and gently kissed her neck.
"I don't understand, Ginny. You're beautiful. Why wouldn't he want to be with you?"
She sighed. "Talk, talk, talk," she said, "and too many questions! He won't find us together in that little bed of yours out there in the stable, now will he? And what's all that about? There's a question for you. A false panel behind wild Nell's stall and a bed of straw and blankets at the back of it. And I found your little stash of baccy and rum out there. You're not the only one who can ask questions Tom!"

“I’ve hidden more than a few tubs of spirits in there over the years, Ginny. That little bolthole of mine has helped to save the skins of many a landlord here at Jamaica Inn, and my own along with them from time to time. But when did you discover it? Nell won’t have anyone stay in the stall with her but me.”
“I saw that right enough last night. She kicked the poor chaise driver such a blow in the leg that he fell to the floor. That’s when I noticed the panel. But she let me calm her after he’d gone. Real fond of me she is now. Come out to the stable and I’ll show you. I’d like another look at your little bolthole, as you call it. And you’ll make love to me out there or I’ll not tell you the truth about why Jim married me.”
“When’s the stage due in?” he asked her.
“Not ‘til mid-morning,” she said, unwinding her arms from around his neck and grabbing his hands as she made for the door.
“Time enough then,” he replied.

Soon after Tom had walked away from Hele Farm that morning, Jon and William Allen had gone outside together to the yard to tend their livestock.
“We’ve got company son.” William had noticed a horse and rider behind the house, in the lane that led away between their fields to turn and join up with the turnpike road in front of the inn.

The visitor turned out to be a rider from Trelawne who asked if he could rest his horse for a while

before he set out again across the moor on his return journey to Looe.
"I have a letter in my saddlebag from Sir Harry Trelawny," he told them, "addressed to a Mr William Allen, a Mr Jon Allen and a man by the name of Tombar."
"Well, we are William and Jon Allen. Tombar is not here right now, but he does live with us."
"I believe you knew Miss Annabelle Trelawny?" The messenger was looking directly at William, who shook his head.
"No, not me, but Tombar and my son here know her well. Many years back they attended her wedding in Surrey. They always rode over to see her whenever she returned to Trelawne, but she hasn't been well enough to travel to Cornwall for some time now."
"It's not good news Mr Allen. I'm afraid she's passed away."

Jon paled and turned towards the inn. "Tom should know. I must tell him straight away."
"He'll know soon enough Jon. Take this poor man inside for now while I see to his horse. Make us all a drink son. Something stronger than tea I think. And rouse Amy from her bed."
William turned to their visitor. "Jon's wife is the only one amongst us who can read this letter. She's not been well but I know she'll want to meet you. Follow Jon to the kitchen and you can tell us why Sir Harry saw fit to send you across the moor after nightfall. It seems a very strange thing for him to do. We could have waited a few more hours for this

news if it meant you're travelling the moor under safer circumstances."
"Well that's not too difficult to explain Mr Allen. Our Sir Harry does seem a little strange. Some go as far as to call him 'mad Sir Harry'. He inherited Trelawne about five years back, a mere lad of sixteen at the time. He's already destroyed all of the beautiful gardens, drained the lily ponds and had the fountains taken away. Turned it all into parkland. And he's had the old gatehouse knocked down. It wouldn't have crossed his mind that I might be in any danger, crossing the moor in the dead of night. Luckily I am familiar with the safe ways to cross the moor after dark, if you know what I mean Mr Allen. Not that Sir Harry knows that about me of course. But we've all got a hand in this smuggling game these days, haven't we? Young Sir Harry's more than willing to buy a bit of contraband if it comes his way. The old Bishop would turn in his grave if he knew what was going on at Trelawne nowadays."

"There's no one about," Tom called and Ginny joined him as he opened the half stable door. They ran across the yard and into the inn, arms wrapped around each other as they stumbled through the kitchen door, completely unaware that they were no longer alone.
"Tell me this isn't what I think it is. This day is going from bad to worse!"
"Jon! What's happened? Why are you here?"

"I came up to talk to you, but that was hours ago. Bad news my friend. It's Miss Annabelle. We've had word that she's passed away."

Tom sat down heavily in the nearest seat. There were tears in his eyes and he seemed unable to speak. Jon pulled a chair across to sit beside him, and for a while the two men sat in silence as Ginny stood watching the fire slowly die away on the hearth. She crossed the room and crouched down in front of it, trying to breathe life back into the smouldering peat, with the little bellows that normally worked so well.

"Who was Miss Annabelle?" she asked and Tom cleared his throat before answering her.

"She was a very special woman, Ginny. She gave me the courage to run away from slavery. I'll tell you about her one day." He turned to Jon. "How did you hear of her death?"

"A rider came over from Trelawne early this morning. He told us, and he brought a letter from Sir Harry Trelawny, addressed to the three of us Tom, to you and to me and to my father. We can't open it unless you are there, so I came up to fetch you as soon as I could. Our visitor will be well on his way back across the moor by now."

A little smile crossed his face. "Two men came by in a small chaise while you were outside. Customs men, who would have searched the house if I hadn't plied them with whisky and sent them on their way with that sack of potatoes that you left out in the middle of the floor."

"The potatoes!" Ginny had turned very pale. "Someone is coming to collect those potatoes before nightfall Jon. They were delivered here last night and Tom thought there was something more than potatoes in the sack. He brought them out from the backroom to take a look but I stopped him."

"So, you stopped him did you Ginny? Well you were lucky that I took a look then, before the customs came by." And he delved deep into his pockets, bringing out one large potato from either side of his coat. "I reckon these are what your man will be after when he comes around at nightfall."

Tom took one of them from him and turned it over in his hand. "It's been cut clean in half and wired back together," he said.

Ginny scrambled up from the floor in front of the fire. A little flame miraculously shot out of the smouldering peat.

"This one's the same," Jon smiled again. "I cleaned them all up a little and it was clear these were different from the rest," he said. "So while the customs men were busy drinking whisky in the bar, I came out to the kitchen and popped them into my pockets."

"I've seen this before Jon. Do you know what's inside?"

"Precious stones. Diamonds I think, but I'm no expert. Take a look, but we must get these down to the farm and dirty the skins up again, hide them away in another sack of potatoes and bring them back for Ginny to hand over to whoever comes for them at nightfall. They'll never know the difference.

But we could all be in an early grave if these men don't get their diamonds tonight."

"This is why Jim didn't want me up here last night. He didn't want me knowing that he was smuggling diamonds. If he'd only put more trust in me we wouldn't be in this mess."

"Poor man. If he had but known, he could trust you with all of his darkest secrets, couldn't he Tom? But he can't trust you with his wife. What's the matter with you man? He'll kill you both if he catches you out. And where is he now? That's what I'd like to know. Leaving Ginny alone to deal with God knows who in the middle of the night."

"He thought he'd be back Jon," Ginny said quietly. "He told me he'd be back, but now I'm thinking that maybe he's been murdered for what he knew about these diamonds. I can't bear this Jon. I think the world of Jim and he would never hurt a hair on my head, whatever you think of him. And he wouldn't care about me and Tom neither." Jon shook his head in disbelief, but Tom slapped him gently on the back.

"There'll be a stage through soon Jon. Help us to get that one on its way. God willing, none of the passengers will want to stay the night and we'll all be able to walk down to the farm together. I'll not leave Ginny alone here ever again. She's with me now and there'll be no consequences Jon. We'll explain it all while we cross the fields, and you'll understand I promise you."

It had been easier for Ginny, telling Jon Allen about her life before she'd given herself to Tom. Firstly, she hadn't really cared what he'd thought of her; she had known that Tom believed her and that was all that had mattered to her as they'd all three trudged across the fields on their way to Hele Farm. Secondly, she hadn't had to look into Jon's face as she clung on tightly to Tom's arm and looked down, watching the rough ground beneath her feet. It had been easier then telling Tom.

"My father was a brute," she'd said, "he knocked us all about, my mother, my sisters and my little brother. He near killed my mother once, punching her so hard that she fell down the stairs. I was the youngest of my sisters, and they all got themselves married as soon as they were old enough. I didn't know why at the time, but I know now right enough. I was fifteen when he came to me one day in our kitchen, told me to get up to my bed and he was coming up to show me what my husband would do to me when I was married. He didn't think I'd have the nerve to run out of the house, but I did. We lived in a terrace of cottages see, and Jim lived next to us. I ran straight in through his door and hid away. Jim had been a good friend to us, even to my dad, but he'd always known what was going on in our house. When he found me there, he said that I could stay with him for a while, he'd sort it out, he said. But my dad came banging on his door after a week, saying that the neighbours were talking about us, and I'd have to go home with him. Well, Jim put his arm around my shoulder, bold as brass he was, told my dad that he was going to marry me, so I wasn't going home with him, not ever. And that's what he did. Married me. But it's not a proper marriage. He told me from the start that he wasn't going to lay a finger on me. He's got a woman see, in Halworthy, where we come from. She's married, got a few little ones by her husband, but he's away at sea for months at a time. Her youngest is Jim's, but she's never told her old man.

I can leave Jim whenever I want, he's always said that. But I've never wanted to leave him. He's a good man and we've been together six years. I was happy to come out here to the inn with him. He worked at Halworthy Inn, same as my mother did when I was small. She used to clean for them. Jim worked in the bar, but he wanted something more for himself. A place of his own; but now I'm thinking that he won't be coming back, and I can't bear it. He could be lying dead out there on the moor, and all for a few diamonds. But if he does come back, he'll let me go with Tom, once he knows that's what I want."

She'd fallen silent, still watching her feet as they'd paced across the field, one, two, three… ten paces before Jon had placed his hand on her shoulder. It had been hard for him, knowing what he'd thought of her before he'd heard her story. Words weren't enough, and so he'd kept his hand on her shoulder until they'd reached the farm house.

William had met them at the door. "What kept you Jon? We were worried. And Mrs Rodda? Come in my dear. Mary we have a guest."

Mary had been sat at the table, several pieces of paper spread out in front of her; her hand up to her mouth as she stared at Ginny.
"It's all right my dear, nothing for you to worry about, but Mr Rodda has disappeared. He didn't come back last night, so we thought it best if his wife came down with us. It's not safe for her up at the inn on her own. Not at the moment. But it's all a very long story, so we won't go into it right now."
Jon had crossed the room to sit beside his wife, and look at the papers on the table.

"We've opened the letter, son. I'm sorry Tom, but it was addressed to the three of us and Mary thought that it might take her some time to read it."
"I can't read well," Mary had said faintly, "and I thought the letter might contain long words and be difficult for me to understand."
"And was it difficult?" Tom had asked, ushering Ginny to the table and sitting her down between himself and Mary.
William had joined them. "Not for Mary," he'd said, "it turned out that it was all quite easy for her to read. But I'm afraid that I have found the letter very difficult to understand."
"You father? But why? What does it say in this letter?"
William had sighed, but said nothing more, and so Mary had picked up the papers and arranged them in order.
"I won't read out every word," she'd said, running her finger across the lines, "but the letter is from Sir Harry Trelawny, who inherited the manor five years

ago. He says that it is with regret that he has to inform you of the recent passing of Mrs Annabelle Squires, formerly Miss Annabelle Trelawny, widow of Sir Charles Squires, of Godolphin House, Guilford in Surrey. He then says that you are each to receive a substantial amount of money from Mrs Squires, and that one of the small terrace of cottages that are to be built close by to Jamaica Inn will be Tom's. It seems that she has supplied all of the money for the cottage that is nearest to the inn to be built, and that Tom is to inherit that cottage from her. But you are all to go to Trelawne in the New Year for the reading of the will, and to receive personal letters from Mrs Squires which are not, as yet, in Sir Harry's possession."

"I don't really understand all of this either," Tom had said. "I'll be more than happy to own that cottage, especially since it's a gift from Miss Annabelle, but why has she been so generous to us when she had a family who were so good to her before she married. She had nieces and nephews who were very dear to her. She did enough for me before I left Trelawne and I hadn't expected any more. I wasn't really family to her."

"You are mistaken Tom," William had said, "you were as dear to her as any of her family, and as it turns out, Jon and myself, are also a part of her family, the Trelawnys, and that is why I am finding all of this so very difficult. Mary, could you read the rest of the letter to all of us please. I think that would be the easiest way of saying this."

"Well, Sir Harry writes here at the end, that Mrs Squires wanted you all to know, before the reading of the will, that William Allen was her natural son, and that Jake Allen was his natural father. It seems that she has explained everything in her personal letters and prays that you will not judge her or Jake too harshly."

"How can I not judge them?" William had asked bitterly, "especially my father."

"If I have learned anything from this day it is that we should not judge anyone until we know the truth behind their story." Jon had smiled at Ginny. "We always knew father, you and I, that your own mother couldn't keep you, and that Sir Jonathon had given you to Jake and Kath Allen to bring up as their own son. Now we know that your mother was my, and Tom's Miss Annabelle, who gave you up to be raised by your own father. It's hard to believe, I'll give you that, but it means that we have roots now, right here on Hele Farm. We are Allens and Trelawnys. That's something to be proud of. Let's wait and see what Miss Annabelle has to say to us in her letters before we start judging any of our family."

"Do you think it's too late to find out who your parents are, Mrs Allen?" Ginny had asked.

"My parents? I was raised by my parents on Gilbert Farm in Halworthy. Their name was Hocken. David and Elizabeth Hocken."

"No, I meant your real parents. I know who raised you, Mrs Allen. My mother found you lying on a bed, newborn and wrapped up in blankets at the

Halworthy Inn. That's how I know. She might have kept you herself if my father hadn't been such a brute. *'My little foundling'*, she used to call you. She knew Mrs Hocken was still nursing her youngest, so she took you to Gilbert Farm to see if she would feed you. That's how the Hockens came to bring you up. My mother heard as how you'd married Mr Allen after Mr Hocken died. Real pleased for you she was. Oh, I hope I've not upset anyone."

They'd all been looking at her, completely astonished and shocked by her words.
"Are you sure of this Ginny?" Jon had taken Mary's hand in his.
"Sure as I'm sat here worrying about Jim and those potatoes in your pockets," she'd said.
"Then it's the best news we've had in a very long time. Isn't it my dear?" Jon had said, kissing his wife soundly on the lips. "This has been an incredible day, but unfortunately it hasn't ended yet." He had dug deeply into his coat pockets, bringing out the two potatoes. "It looks as if Ginny's husband may have got himself mixed up with diamond smugglers. These potatoes each contain several small diamonds and we need to get them back up to the inn. Someone is coming for them just before nightfall. It will be best if you stay here with Mary for a while Ginny. I'm sure my wife has a lot of questions for you. Do you know much about babies my dear?"
"Well I've had none of my own, but my sisters all have children. I looked after their little ones many a time when I lived in Halworthy."

"Then you two have enough to talk about to last a lifetime. Come on Tom, we have to get moving. Father, we need you with us, and a couple of shotguns, just to be on the safe side. But first we need a sack of potatoes to hide these in."
"A sack of potatoes? Surely they came already hidden in sack of potatoes!"
"They did father, but the customs men have them, along with a couple of poor Jim's bottles of whisky. As I said, it's been an incredible day. But I'll tell you all about it while we walk back across the fields, and Tom will explain to you why it took us all so long to return to the farm this morning, but you'll understand father. I can promise you that!"

The potatoes containing the diamonds were once more heavily disguised, and hidden in the centre of a sack of potatoes to be taken to Jamaica Inn. Bearing the weight of the heavy sack on their backs, the three men shared the task of carrying it across the fields, but it was Jon, balancing the sack on the top of his shoulders, who led the way through the passage beside the cow byre, and into the yard in front of the inn.

"Well, well, Mr Allen, I see that you have brought another sack of potatoes for me. I suspect that these are the ones that I was looking for earlier today."
Shocked by the sight of one of the customs men who'd been at the inn that morning, Jon stopped in the entrance to the passageway and lowered the sack to the ground. "I am merely replacing the potatoes that I allowed you to take away, sir. We have more

than enough for our own needs on the farm. I brought these up for Mrs Rodda."

"Mrs Rodda is not here and it seems that her husband hasn't returned either. In fact I've carried out a thorough search and found no-one anywhere, in or around the house. I didn't suspect you of anything when we met this morning Mr Allen. You explained that you had walked up from your farm to see the innkeeper, and that you were quite worried that there was no-one around, either in the house or in any of the outbuildings. We took you at your word sir, my fellow officer and myself, and we left here fairly certain that we had in our possession a sack of potatoes which also contained some form of contraband. We were in the Royal Hotel in Bodmin in the early hours of the morning you see Mr Allen, at the time when the mail coach arrived, and we overheard the driver telling someone in the stables that there was something going on at the Jamaica Inn. The innkeeper was not at home he said, just his slip of a wife, and no-one in the stables to help him change his horses either. Apparently there is a wild horse in one of the stalls that kicked him in the leg, and knocked him to the ground. He was an angry man, Mr Allen, but it was when he mentioned meeting a man with a horse and cart on the road, soon after he had left the inn, that he aroused our suspicions. *'A man with a horse, and a cart with a single sack on it',* he said, *"out in the dead of the night and heading towards the inn."*

"Well I know nothing more than I told you this morning." Jon said, "May I ask what you found in

those potatoes that brought you back here on your own and with so little delay?"
"I found nothing at all Mr Allen. I am on my own because the landlord at the Royal offered us a drink, ale or spirits, much as you did sir, and my companion chose to drink himself senseless, while I returned to the chase to search through the sack. But it contained nothing but potatoes, and that's what led me to suspect that you had already found and removed the contraband. I knew that if I waited for my friend to be fit enough to travel with me, I would lose any chance of finding out what was going on here at the inn, and of seizing any possible smuggled goods."
He was looking over Jon's shoulder, distracted by some movement in the passageway.
"But I can see that you are not alone Mr Allen. Would you kindly step aside, so that I can see your companion?"

Jon stood firm, but William came out to face the man who was challenging his son.
"I understood that a sack of potatoes was being collected before nightfall," he said. "That is why we are replacing them."
"And is that why you thought fit to bring a shotgun with you sir?" The customs officer pulled out one of the pistols from the belt around his coat, and levelled it at William's head. "Now drop that gun, kick it over here and bring that sack into the kitchen. I want to see what's in there before I take it away."
William glanced at Jon before kicking the shotgun over to the customs officer. "However this may look

to you my man, we are not guilty of any wrong doings here. We are farmers, not smugglers."

Following closely behind them, the barrel of the pistol pressed firmly into the back of William's neck, the customs officer escorted William and Jon into the kitchen, as together they carried the sack and dropped it onto the table.
"Now sit down here please sirs, side by side in front of me, and take those potatoes out, one at a time, so that I can see each of them clearly."
Having little choice in the matter, they followed his orders and began to empty the sack, both furtively avoiding the wired potatoes; knowing that they were delaying the inevitable, but praying that any delay would give Tom the opportunity to help them. Though what he could do to free them, and then clear their names once the diamonds were discovered, they couldn't begin to imagine.

With his back to the granite wall of the inn, between the stables and the open kitchen window, Tom waited, listening in on the guarded conversation between his friends and the young customs officer. He was well armed, with William's shotgun from the farm and his own pistol, which he kept hidden from prying eyes behind Wild Nell's stall. But as he made a move and crouched down to pass unnoticed below the window, he was praying that the customs officer would once more take Jon at his word, and free the father and son who had so innocently got caught up in this plot to smuggle diamonds across the county, using Jamaica Inn as a stopping point on their journey towards a destination much further up the country.

As he straightened up again on the other side of the window, he realised to his dismay that he was no longer alone. The driver of a horse and small cart had arrived outside of the inn on the Launceston side of the turnpike road, previously hidden from view by the long row of outhouses and barns, and too close to the buildings to be spotted by anyone inside the house.
'Someone is coming to collect those potatoes before nightfall.' Ginny's, and, more recently, William's words echoed around in Tom's head. The smuggler, no doubt armed himself, had turned up for his precious contraband, to be greeted by the sight of a black man with a pistol and a shotgun, sneaking around towards the entrance to the inn.

The stranger though was frowning, nothing but concern on his strangely familiar face, and although Tom held up his hand to warn him to stay away, the man dismounted from his seat at the front of the cart and crossed the yard to join him beside the window.
"Tom?" he asked, his voice reduced to a whisper, "Tombar from Trelawne?" Without waiting for an answer he grasped Tom's arm. "Reg Clemo's son," he said softly, "I'm Jack Clemo."
Tom sank to the ground in relief.
"Have you come for potatoes?" he asked, and Jack nodded. "They're in there," Tom gestured towards the window, "with two of my friends and a man from the customs. He has a gun to their heads."

“Let me see that one!” the customs officer said sharply as Jon pulled out an earthy potato, clearly bound up with thin wire, from amongst a handful that were left in the sack. Jon held it up, hoping the man would reach forward to take it; giving him the opportunity to knock the pistol from his other hand.
“I’ll need you to open it Mr Allen. You’ll not catch me off guard in that way!”
Taking it from his son, William removed the wire and split the potato in half, revealing the precious little stones that were nestling inside.
“Diamonds, Mr Allen! So you are not as innocent as you would have had me believe. And no doubt there are more inside the sack. So what am I to do now? I should arrest you, seize these gems and turn them in to my superiors. Or I could shoot you both and keep them for myself. You would be discovered and thought murdered by smugglers, any contraband spirited away across the moor and lost for ever. No-one would suspect me. I would merely say that I returned to Jamaica Inn and found it deserted. No loose ends.”
“Just one sir. You have forgotten the murdering smugglers!” It was Jack who spoke. In a panic the officer swung around to face the men who had crept up so silently behind him, their guns aimed steadily at his chest. Targeting Tom with his pistol, he pulled a second from his belt and hurriedly fired both, but Jon had turned in his seat to push the man, and as the officer lost his balance, two more shots rang out, and he fell to the floor at their feet.

"Is he dead?" Tom asked, clutching his leg and sinking down into a chair.
"Stone dead. Two shots to the chest." Jon was leaning over the man whose blood was spreading across the surface of the slated floor.
"He would have killed us all," Jack said, staring at Jon as he spoke. "You're Jon Allen! I thought I recognised you! I'm Jack Clemo. I was only a lad when you helped put out the fire at Trelawne. You were heroes to me. You and Tom here."
"Can we trust you then, Jack Clemo?" William asked. "Because between us we've killed a man today, and not just any man!"
"You can all trust me with your lives sir, though I'm ashamed to say that I'm the man you were expecting to come for those potatoes, and I must take them and the diamonds with me, or my life won't be worth living. My home's not at Trelawne anymore, not since Sir Harry inherited. I live in Launceston now, and that's where I've to deliver that contraband, though I didn't know I would be carrying diamonds sir, I swear, not until I heard that officer say it, when we were outside by the window."
"Then we'll bag up the potatoes again and send you on your way Jack. You don't need to be involved in what happens next here today."
"His horse and chaise are around the far side of the long barn sir, I saw them there as I came close to the inn. You'll have to lose them out on the moor, but I'd be obliged if you take them farther down on the road towards Bodmin. Throw any suspicion as far away as possible from any of us up at Launceston. The excise will think their man taken by smugglers."

"No loose ends!" Tom stood up and limped over to look at the man lying dead on the kitchen floor.
"You're injured my friend!" Jack exclaimed, noticing the brief grimace of pain that had shot across Tom's face as he'd pushed himself up from the chair.
"A flesh wound, nothing serious. But I may not have fared so well if this man had hit his target."
"Better clean it and bind it though, Tom," William said. "And I'll come up with Jon to see to the post in the night. We can't risk the mail man knowing you've been injured. There'll be enough idle talk about the disappearance of a customs man, without you getting caught up in it."

They buried him in the dead of night, six feet under, beside a gnarled and stunted old oak that had watched over the middle field between the Jamaica Inn and Hele Farm for as long as anyone could remember. The horse and chaise which had been his transport to the inn, earlier in the day, took his body to its resting place, along the lane between the turnpike road and Hele Farm, the lane that had brought the messenger from Trelawne to the farm house, at the dawn of that same incredible day.
"It's best he's here on our land," William said, as they carried the body between the chaise and the grave that they had already dug out for him. "They'll build on to the inn over the years, but they won't come out as far as this field."

“Should we take his clothes and burn them?” Jon asked his father. “Without that uniform no-one would ever know who this man was.”
“No-one will find him here son. Not while any of us are alive, or any of our young’uns for that matter. Leave him with his uniform and his guns. If this body is ever discovered, it will be too late to lay blame on any living soul.”

Chapter Five

Winter 1863

Emily Polkinhorne stood watching, as the snow fell thick and fast outside her window; dry, heavy flakes that soon began to stick, catching the slate roofs of the old stables and the cow byre on the far side of the road that ran between her cottage and the Jamaica Inn. A pile of logs beside the inn's ancient door, and even the mountings of its gently swinging sign, began to disappear beneath a little topping of snow.

Her end cottage, one of a small terrace that had been built almost one hundred years before, was the closest to the inn, and although she'd lived there throughout the whole of her long life, the comings and goings across the road still fascinated her. On this particular winter's day though, as the snowfall steadily thickened, and deadened any sound from the coach and horses that were slowly turning into the yard of the coaching inn, there was another event, finally unfolding its secret and holding her spellbound. Suddenly time had seemed to slow, almost to a standstill, and everything around her fell gently into place.

She had been watching the two small boys, pacing up and down in the road outside for most of the day. Her grandson, Harry Reskelly and his only young friend, Joe Allen, both unusually quiet and serious, whispering together, thoughtfully watching the darkening sky and so engrossed in their plotting and planning that they had forgotten to come in for their mid-day bread and dripping.

The boys were sat facing each other in the road, cross-legged and solemn faced, the snow falling around them, clinging to their hair and shoulders as Joe pulled a rusty old penknife from his trouser pocket and carefully unfolded the blade. Harry, steadying his own left wrist with his right hand, held out his thumb and waited for the cut. Flinching slightly as the blade sliced into his flesh, he watched his blood flow unchecked across the surface of his skin, before taking the penknife from his friend. The process was repeated, this time on Joe's upturned hand. Harry produced a handkerchief from his coat pocket and, arms held high, they bound their wounded thumbs together, waiting until a crimson spot appeared staining the grubby material.
"Blood brothers!"
Slowly they both turned their heads towards her, as if they had known all along that she would be watching. Broad smiles spread across their faces as they scrambled to their feet, and Harry's stained handkerchief fell unnoticed onto the snow. Time

gathered pace again, returning to normal as they ran towards her cottage and hurtled in through the open door.

As Emily watched from her doorway, a swift shaft of light from the brightening skies struck one of the inn's bedroom windows; the window of the bedroom nearest to her cottage; the bedroom where the boys had both been born. Emily smiled and closed the door behind her.

"And who put that little idea into your heads?" she asked, as the boys sat together at the table. "Blood brothers indeed, when the pair of you are closer than any brothers I've ever come upon!"

"But we weren't real brothers, were we Gran?" Harry said, examining the cut on his thumb. "Not before."

"We are now though." Joe left the table to look out of the window. "We should walk down to the farm, show my mother what we've done. She said Harry could come to tea. We're having mutton stew."

"Well mutton stew or no mutton stew, you're not going anywhere just yet." Emily frowned. "You can't see your hand in front of your face out there. Come back to the table Joe. I'll make us all a nice pot of tea."

"Can't we just go over to the inn and tell Mr Trenchard. He'll be really pleased." Harry jumped up from his chair and joined Joe at the window.

"That old reprobate! Bill Trenchard. So he put you up to this did he? I might have guessed."

"It wasn't his idea," Joe said, "not really. I heard my brothers talking about it, but it was Mr Trenchard said we had to wait for the snow. *'That's what puts the magic into it,'* he said. *'Makes you real brothers for ever and a day.'"*

"Silly old fool," she said, "but he's as fond of you boys as he is of that inn over there, I'll give him that. But he won't be supping ale over there yet a while Harry. He'll be next door with his wife and looking out of his window, same as you I shouldn't wonder."
"Joe was born in the winter, when it was snowing like it is today," Harry said, "and I was born in the summer, when it was hot and sunny. Tell us again how we came to be born over in the inn."
"I've told you that story a dozen times," Emily said, "you both know it inside out."
"I'll tell it then," Harry nudged Joe's arm and they both returned to the table. "Mr Dunn was the innkeeper in January in 1855," he said, starting the story in the same way that his grandmother always told it. "And that year we had a very bad winter out here on Bodmin Moor. Every day was icy cold and everywhere was slippery under foot. Mrs Dunn took ill and was too poorly to leave her bed, so for a few days Mr Dunn cooked breakfast for the travellers who stayed overnight, until one morning, he went outside to bring in a log for the fire, and he slipped over. He couldn't move his arm at all. Proper swollen it was, but he had meals to make and sheets to change and a big stage coach due in by mid-morning. So he walked down across the fields to see if Mrs Allen could come up to help him."

Harry paused and looked across the table at his grandmother.

"You tell it now, Gran," he said. "You tell this next bit better than me, and you always remember something new that you haven't told us before. We want to hear it from you, don't we, Joe?"

Joe nodded eagerly, so Emily gave in and continued the story.

"Well Mrs Allen, Joe's mother, was expecting our Joe here, but she didn't think that he would be born that day, and she went straight back up to the inn with Thomas Dunn to help out. It was as they were crossing the last field, the little meadow right behind the inn, that they noticed little flakes of snow drifting down around them. Mr Dunn didn't think it would settle, and your mother wasn't too worried either Joe. We see a fair bit of snow out here in the winter, but it's usually gone again before nightfall. It was a different story though by the time the stage arrived. The sky had turned black and every grassy hill and craggy tor around the inn was covered in a blanket of thick snow. That light flurry of flakes had turned into a blizzard. The stage driver was anxious to change horses and get on his way into Bodmin while the road was still passable, but Thomas Dunn was in so much pain from his arm that the task was beyond him. Two of the men in the coach turned out to help, and your mother, bless her, joined them, but it was right then Joe, in the middle of all that cursing and chaos that you decided to come into the world. They managed to get her up into that little end bedroom, nearest to this cottage, and it was clear, or so they said afterwards, that you were in a real hurry to join them. But something was wrong, and your mother was in a great deal more pain than she'd ever been in when your older brothers were born. Someone was looking out for you that day though Joe. Someone or something was looking out for your whole family that day. One of the passengers on that stage was a doctor, and when he knew that your mother was having trouble giving birth to you, he told the stage driver to go on his way into Bodmin with his passengers, before the blizzard left them all stranded at the inn. That doctor saved your lives Joe, yours and your mother's. He realised that you were coming into this world sideways, and he managed to turn you; deliver you the right way around. He stayed there in that bedroom with your mother until she'd fed you and fallen asleep, and while all this had been going on, the snow had turned to rain and the turnpike road was clear again. When the mail coach came through in the night, that doctor climbed up front with the driver and continued on his way into Bodmin. Next morning Jon Allen's great-great grandson was alive and safe in his mother's arms in that little bedroom over there, in Jamaica Inn. Your father tried to trace the man who'd saved the lives of his wife and son, but no one had thought to ask his name, and he was never seen again, not out here at the inn or in Bodmin for that matter. There was a little bit of magic around that day, Joe."

"So Joe was coming into the world sideways." Harry's dark eyes were shining as he looked up at his grandmother. "Did you just remember that Gran? You told us before that the doctor saved their lives,

but you never said anything about coming into the world sideways!"
"Maybe I didn't think you were old enough to hear it until now." Emily said, pushing back her chair and getting up from the table. "I'll make us that pot of tea."
"We'll be eight next year," Joe was saying, as she spooned tea into the pot and poured boiling water in from the kettle that simmered continuously over the peat fire. "Same age as your great-great grandfather was when he stowed away on a ship in Jamaica to come to Cornwall."
"Tell us about him, Gran. Tell us something new about Tombar when he was growing up."
"There's nothing new to tell, Harry," she said, bringing a tray with cups, milk and tea to the table. "I've told you all I know about him before he came to live here in this cottage."
"Did Ginny's husband ever come back?" Joe asked. "Did she marry Tombar?"
"She married him Joe, in the little church in Blisland, but I'm not sure if it was all above board and legal. In those days the Vicar would marry anyone if they paid him enough. I don't suppose it mattered much anyway. Jim Rodda never came back, and Ginny was sure that he'd been murdered for what he knew about those diamonds."
"And this cottage will be mine one day." Harry said, looking around the cosy kitchen.
"It certainly will my, boy." Emily ruffled his black curls. "You've no worries there. I've made sure of it. It may only be one room down and one up, but it will be all yours one day. The others can never lay

their hands on it. They deserted you and left me to bring you up. So what's mine will be yours. There are papers in at the solicitors in Launceston, with a Mr Peter and his son, setting it all straight for you."
"Where did they go, Gran?" Harry had never asked that before and she knew there would be more questions to follow as the years went by. He'd had a mother, a father and three sisters, and lost them all on the day he was born. But she'd always been honest with him. She'd seen no sense in spinning yarns when someone would be sure to tell him the truth one day. Better he knew it from the start.
"I wish I knew, Harry," she said. " One day we might find out where they are, but for now all we have is the story of the day you were born, so I'll tell that to you again now, if you want me to."
The boys both nodded happily and so Emily filled the three cups with milk, and tea from the pot, before sitting down to tell a very different story.

"Your father, Daniel Reskelly, was a farm worker on Two Barrows land. You can see the farmhouse from behind the inn, way over on the opposite side to Hele Farm. He married our daughter Flo when she'd just turned twenty. We were only blessed with the one youngster, though we wanted more. But Flo and Daniel had three daughters, your sisters, Ada, Win and little Florrie, and most Sundays they'd all walk over here for their dinner. Not that we ever saw much of your father. Most of his day would be spent drinking over at the inn. The summer you were born we had a real hot spell of weather, and this one Sunday in July, when Flo was expecting you to arrive any day, and Daniel was across at the inn, your older sisters came into the cottage saying that they couldn't find little Florrie anywhere. Your mother was beside herself Harry, and we all searched high and low until Flo decided to fetch your father back from the inn, to help look for her. She was afraid, you see, that Florrie may have wandered out onto the moor. Well she'd only just got inside the inn door when she realised that you were on the way. The girls had all been born quickly, no time at all from start to finish, so she thought it best not to come back to the cottage, and Mrs Dunn took her up over the stairs to the same bedroom that you were born in, Joe, only six months before. Your father had followed them upstairs and he was there in the room when Mrs Dunn delivered you. She told me afterwards that she'd been so happy for them, having a boy after the three girls, but then they all realised that you were black, and Mrs Dunn, poor soul, didn't know what to say to them. She didn't know that Flo's great-grandfather had been an African slave who'd come to Cornwall from Jamaica more than a hundred years before. All she could think of was that Flo had been messing around with some other man, and that this baby boy that she was wrapping up in a blanket to give to its mother, wasn't Daniel Reskelly's son."

"Harry's not really black though, is he Mrs Polkinghorne?" Joe interrupted Emily, swilling the tea around in his cup. "He's more the colour of tea when you mix it up with milk."

Emily stared at him and started to laugh. "There's more truth in that than I think you realise, Joe," she said, "and I wish someone had said that very thing to Harry's father that day, it might have made him see sense. Daniel had always known about Tombar, right from when he first started courting our Flo. She'd told him that if they married and had children, there was a chance they could be black like her great-grandfather. But I don't suppose he thought it would happen, not with so many generations in between." She paused. There was such a sorrowful expression on Harry's young face that she wondered if she should leave the story there, and let the boys go outside for a while to enjoy their special day in the snow. It wasn't as if Harry didn't know how the story ended.

Luckily, Joe solved the problem for her. "And he walked out of the room and out of the inn and was never seen again," he said, scraping his chair on the slate floor as he got up from the table and ran over to the window.

"Well, not by me anyway, Joe," Emily said, "but a while after he'd gone, Flo brought little Harry over to the cottage. She thought he might have come over here to see if we'd found Florrie, but we hadn't seen hide nor hair of him, and we all settled down to wait for him to come back. We'd found Florrie upstairs under my bed, fast asleep. The girls were all excited over having a baby brother, but Flo was quiet and I could see she was worrying about Daniel. When he hadn't come back by nightfall, I made up beds for them down here by the fire and took Florrie up to sleep beside me. But when I woke in the morning it was Harry by my side in the bed. They'd gone, taken little Florrie and put Harry in her place, left me to bring him up on my own, with my Stan only passing over not twelve months before. And we've not set eyes on them since, but we've managed well enough haven't we Harry?" She ruffled his hair again.

"The snow's stopped, Mrs Polkinghorne," Joe said, jumping up and down impatiently.
"Well run along with you then. Pop in to the inn and show Bill Trenchard what you've done to those thumbs of yours. No doubt he'll give you both a penny or two for your trouble. And then go on down to the farm for your mutton stew."
Harry's eyes were shining again.
"I'd be happier if your oldest brother William would walk back up with him after tea Joe," Emily said as she went with them to the door. "I don't trust this weather. But tell him not to go filling Harry's head with those ghost stories of his."
"There is a ghost in the middle field between the farm and the inn Mrs Polkinghorne. William says it follows everyone who walks through there."
"Be off with you," she said. "I'm cold standing here in this doorway. Next thing you'll be telling me it's poor Jim Rodda wandering about out there."

The boys laughed and set off through the snow, knowing that she would watch them until they had disappeared through the inn's ancient entrance.

Quietly shutting the heavy door, they crept into the bar, hoping to surprise the man who sat in his favourite chair, facing the fire with his back towards them.
"So what do you think of this weather then, boys?" Bill Trenchard asked as the fire suddenly spat flames through the smouldering peat, and little sparks showered around the hearth."

Chapter Six

1876

When Samuel Carter and his wife Eve moved into Jamaica Inn as its new tenants, they were warned that there had been several highway robberies, close by to the inn on the turnpike road, over the previous two years.
'Nothing regular, nothing to really worry about,' they'd been told. *'Just five or six robberies over the winter and then nothing for months on end.'*

Samuel had thought it strange, as highway robberies had died a natural death more than fifty years before, when stage and mail coach companies had regularly employed armed guards to ride up front with their drivers, and lone travellers were more than likely to be carrying their own repeating revolvers. Samuel though was himself no stranger to crime, and, as a precaution against the appearance of the elusive highwayman, he placed a pistol behind the inn's small bar, and carried another hidden about his person.

He was not a Cornishman, and had only escaped prison some ten years earlier by jumping on to a stage coach bound for Cornwall, and changing his name from Mason to Carter. His crimes had included the handling of stolen goods and the harbouring of criminals at a pub in the East End of London whilst living and working there as the landlord. Escaping to Cornwall, he had travelled as far as Falmouth, where he'd quickly found lodgings close by to the docks with a young widow by the name of Eve Copley, and her nine year old daughter Ellie. Seeking employment in the docks had been his next move, and as a fit man in his late thirties, he'd had no trouble with finding work as a labourer, transferring cargoes on and off the ships that sailed in and out of the port.

His plan to escape from London and the law had apparently been successful, but he hadn't made any plans for what was to happen next in his life. As a confirmed bachelor he hadn't expected to fall in love or indeed to want to get married, but Eve had somehow found her way into his heart, and when he'd told her of his feelings for her, she had admitted to being in love with him from the very first day that he had knocked on her door.

He had been working at the docks for almost ten years and was busy as usual one morning, stacking cargo from a ship just in from Brazil, when he felt, what he later realised was, the inevitable tap on his shoulder.

"Samuel Mason! So this is where you've been hiding yourself! Oh, don't look so alarmed, my man. I've been out of the force for twelve months now. Had enough of working alongside detectives who were as corrupt as the criminals they were attempting to track down. And you are a reformed character by the look of things! Good luck to you Samuel. I must be on my way. Here on business you see. Here on business!"
Throughout the entire meeting, Samuel hadn't uttered a word, but he'd known from the start that his days at Falmouth docks were over. He would have to move on. Detective Sergeant Webber of the City of London Police Force, whether retired or resigned, was not a man to be trusted.

Hearing that the Jamaica Inn on Bodmin Moor was soon to be let to a new tenant, he had applied to take over the lease, and so it had been a Mr Samuel Carter, who at the beginning of May in 1876 had taken up residence at the inn on the moor, along with his wife Eve and step-daughter Ellie.

By that time Eve had been Samuel's wife for more than eight years, and knew enough about her husband's dubious past to willingly agree to leave her home in the busy port of Falmouth with its temperate climate, and move to an isolated area of high moorland where extreme changes of weather and treacherous terrain often made it unthinkable to leave the safety of the few well-travelled roads. To keep the man she loved from being locked up in jail, for crimes he'd committed before she had even known him, Eve Carter would have sailed with him to the ends of the earth.

Joe Allen stood behind the bar at Jamaica Inn, resting his elbows on the counter; running his hands repeatedly through his unruly hair.

"Marry her, boy." Bill Trenchard had been watching Joe, from his favourite seat beside the fire. "I've seen the way she looks at you. She'll have you like a shot. Snap Ellie up before someone else does."

"That's the problem, Bill." Joe groaned as he straightened himself up to look over at the old man who'd been a good friend for so many years. "Harry will be home soon."

"Ah……." Bill supped for a while on his ale. "But Harry wouldn't steal your woman, Joe!"

"He wouldn't mean to. I know that. But what if Ellie takes one look at him and ….. Oh, I know I probably need my head seeing to, Bill, but I have to be sure before I ask her to marry me."

"You do what's right for you then boy, but that girl's yours. Take my word for it. She won't be interested in Harry."

Joe sighed and went back to leaning on the counter; this time with his head in his hands. He still lived down on the farm with his family, but his heart had never been in working on the land. With his father's blessing, he'd spent most of his time helping out at the inn, as his three older brothers were born farmers and more than capable of carrying out all of the work on their land.

Harry Reskelly. The man he called brother, and the man who'd been as close to him as any of his three brothers, William, Ben or Luke. Over the years they had worked together at the inn, and taken their part in the improvements which had changed the original five bedroomed house, with only four rooms downstairs, into a thriving post and coaching house, with eight bedrooms and nine rooms on the lower floor. Both born at the inn, which Harry affectionately called his 'old lady', they had steadily grown alongside it, until two years earlier in the spring of 1874 when Harry's grandmother, Emily Polkinghorne had died; an event which was to change the course of their lives completely.

Shaken, it seemed to the very core by the loss of his grandmother, Harry had packed a few of his belongings into a bag and walked off across the moor towards the coast. He had always been fascinated by tales told at the inn of the lives led by the daring men who went to sea and fished the waters around the Cornish coastline.
'I need to get away from here for a while,' he'd told Joe. *'I'll find a cave to live in and fish off the rocks for my food. Don't worry. As soon as I'm ready to live in the cottage again, I'll come home.'* But spring had turned to summer and summer to autumn, and still Harry had not returned to his home. It wasn't until a fisherman by the name of Robert Wilton had walked into the inn one evening that Joe had finally

discovered where his friend had been for the past few months.

Robert had quite recently come back from Ireland, where he'd been fishing for mackerel with several men from the Looe and Polperro area. He'd told Joe that his brother Peter lived in the old turnpike house at Palmer's Bridge, not a mile from the inn and that he had stayed there quite often over the winter, for the past three years.

"I thought I might find Harry Reskelly here," he'd said. "Would he be over at his cottage?"
When Joe had said that they'd not seen Harry for months, Robert Wilton had seemed surprised.
"Well, he came over with us to Ireland in May, but when we walked off the boat together at Polperro in mid-July, he told me he'd be going straight to his home in Bolventor. He said he lives across the road from here, in the end cottage, nearest to the inn."

When Joe had arrived back at the farm that night, his mother had opened the door to him, her face flushed and smiling.
"Harry's back," she'd said, and Joe could have sworn there were tears in her eyes.

Sitting across the table from Harry in the farmhouse kitchen, Joe had been astonished by the change in his friend's appearance. His normally short and curly hair was much longer, and tied back from a face which had matured and strengthened. There was a quiet confidence about the way he moved, that altered him much more than Joe would ever have believed possible in such a short stretch of time. Harry Reskelly was now a very good looking young man. To talk to though, he was the same old Harry, and they had been so content to be in each other's company again that their banter had continued well into the small hours of the morning.

He had stayed for a few months, enjoying the fuss that Joe's mother had made of him and before long it was as if he had never been away. As winter had begun to set in, work had started less than two miles out on the moor to create an ice works at Dozmary Pool, a shallow natural lake on high ground that had for hundreds of years been a place of mystery and legend. The plan to harvest the thick ice that formed on the lake over the winter months, and store it to pack around the fish that would be taken from Looe to London in warmer weather, had caught Harry's imagination. A deep enclosure had to be hollowed out of the nearby hillside and then lined with granite. This had created more than enough work for willing hands, and Harry had been at the front of the queue.

But spring had followed winter and the call of the sea had lured Harry away from Bolventor once more to fish for his living; this time around the west coast of Scotland in a small mackerel driver. Each time that he had returned to the inn after a long absence, warm flames had risen from the fires to greet him and the women of the ever increasing little community had fussed around him like mother hens. Joe's family had welcomed him back with open arms, and Joe had spent as much time as was possible with his friend, even if it meant occasionally working alongside him in cruelly cold winter temperatures at the ice works. As well, there had been a few precious days, spent on the beaches of Looe and Polperro, sleeping in caves, fishing off the rocks and building little fires to sit around and talk, between mouthful after mouthful of delicious fresh seafood. These days had always been spent together just before Harry had set off on a fishing trip and Joe had then faced a long and lonely walk back across the moor to Bolventor, knowing that his friend wouldn't be in Cornwall again until early autumn, and that he would delay his return home to his cottage in favour of living for a fortnight or more on beaches and in caves once used by bold smugglers who would later trek with their packhorses across the high ground of the moor, to leave their contraband at Jamaica Inn.

'That girl is yours. She won't be interested in Harry.' Bill had seemed very sure of those words. But women seemed to fall under Harry's spell; a spell that Harry himself seemed blissfully unaware of.

Joe had seen four innkeepers come and go in his lifetime, and the latest, Samuel Carter, had moved in with his family almost five months before, not long after Harry had left to go fishing for herrings in Scottish waters. He'd been away for more than five months, far longer than usual, and Joe was expecting him to turn up at the inn any day.

"Joe? Is that you in the bar?" Eve Carter was standing motionless in the middle of the room. "I thought you were a ghost," she said as he straightened up, trying to flatten his wayward hair. "You were so still, so quiet!"
"I'm no ghost, Mrs Carter," Joe came out from behind the counter, "though my brother Will swears this room is haunted."
"I've sensed something in here myself." Eve was looking around, both hands to her heart. "Many's the time I've looked out from behind that bar thinking I've seen a customer come into the room, when there's been no-one in here at all."
"Well I wouldn't worry, Mrs Carter," Joe said anxiously, "There's bound to be a ghost or two around in a house that's been lived in for as many years as this one, what with the smugglers visiting…"

"What's all this talk of ghosts, Joe Allen?" Ellie bustled into the room to interrupt him. "I heard you from the stairs! Frightening my poor mother like that. There's no such thing as ghosts. It's all just stuff and nonsense!"
Joe's eyes lit up as he took Ellie's hand. "Would you like me to introduce you to a ghost, my love?" he said. "If you'll walk out with me tomorrow, I will introduce you to a ghost who will make your hair stand on end."
"I'll do no such thing!" Ellie glared at him, but then glanced hopefully at her mother. A walk alone with Joe was far too tempting to resist.

"Well I can't imagine why you'd want to go out hunting a ghost with Joe, my girl, especially since you've told us that there's no such thing! But I'll not stop you." She smiled to herself as she left them talking to old Bill Trenchard and made her way to the kitchen. No doubt he would have a few ghost stories of his own to tell them.

She liked Joe, the hard working young farmer's son, who had so quickly stolen her daughter's heart. His father and brothers quite often walked up to the inn for a drink at the end of the day, and it was comforting to know that they had such good people close by to call on if there was any trouble. It had amused her recently, to see that the ribbing Joe had always taken so good naturedly from his brother Will, mostly over the way that he chose to earn his living, had all but stopped since he'd had Ellie on his arm. Joe it seemed, had won some serious respect.

She'd only said to Samuel earlier in the day that they would soon be more than grateful for the young man's help, what with having to accommodate the local hunts and feed the large number of sports men who would be turning up at the inn, all expecting a hearty breakfast, before they galloped off in pursuit of some wily old fox.

A sudden commotion had Eve scurrying out of the kitchen to see what all the noise was about. She'd heard the old door slam and someone's angry voice; followed by heavy footsteps in the passageway. A young man was striding out ahead of her towards the bar.

"I've been robbed damn it, and right here on my own father's land!" he exclaimed, looking back at her as she rushed into the room.

"Sit down here, Squire." Bill Trenchard was getting up from his comfortable chair, offering the man a seat. "Young Joe here will get you a drink. Looks like our highwayman has started his antics again, Mrs Carter," Bill said, "tis always around this same time of year."

"Make that a large one for Squire Bray, Joe," Eve said, sitting down beside the young man. It had been his father who had leased the inn to them in the spring, and who owned most of the land around the area. The young Squire had regularly frequented the inn over the summer and had only recently spoken to her about taking the hunting parties, and the possibility of putting up some of the sportsmen over the winter.

"I was on my way to Altarnun to visit with my uncle, when there he was on his horse, just ahead of me in the road, pointing a pistol at my head and demanding my purse. Some damnable man with a mask and a skull cap, dressed more like an old smuggler than a highwayman." The Squire peered up at Joe as he handed him his drink. "Older than you," he said, "thicker set." He sighed, almost as if he'd hoped to find his robber standing there in front of him. "Bloody man. Haunting the road like that. It's not the money though, Mrs Carter. The villain took my wedding ring!"

They all knew that young Squire Bray had only been married a month before, in The Holy Trinity Church just down in the hollow below the inn, near the road towards the west.
"Another brandy for the Squire, Joe, if you will." Eve began to twist her own wedding ring around on her finger. "Would you know him again if you saw him? Or his horse, perhaps you would recognise his horse?"
The young Squire shook his head. "It was too dark to see anything clearly," he said, "and no markings on his horse to speak of. Very ordinary. Just a brown nag."
"Were you very frightened, sir?" Ellie asked, and he looked up in surprise. He hadn't even noticed the pretty girl who now stood beside the bar, clinging tightly to Joe's arm.
"Why no, my dear," he said vaguely, "Not frightened exactly. Shocked, furious, but not frightened." He frowned. "We will all have to be on our guard from now on though, Mrs Carter. You must inform everyone, so that they can defend themselves against this blaggard."

To Ellie's surprise, Joe's walk to introduce her to a ghost had led them around behind the stables, over the little style in the hedge and into the meadow at the back of the inn.
"Are we going down to the farm then?" she asked. "Do you have a ghost in the farmhouse?"

Joe put his hand to her lips. "No more talk of ghosts, Ellie. Not now. Just walk beside me for a while longer."
It was as they approached the middle field between the inn and the farmhouse that Ellie felt the menacing change in the air around her. She kept walking, but slowly, reaching out for Joe's coat to pull him back beside her. Too afraid to even look around, she fixed her eyes on the distant farmhouse and tightened her grip on his coat.
"That bad eh?" Joe murmured, sensing her discomfort and throwing his arm around her shoulders. "We'll have to get him used to you then! It gets better Ellie, everyone says it gets easier to cross the field as time goes by. It's as if he mellows a little when he knows who you are. It's always been alright for me. I don't know why. Will thinks it's because I first crossed the field on the day I was born, carried across in my mother's arms. We'll turn around and go back now, if you want to. It'll be quicker than passing by the old tree and walking across the field to the lane."

Ellie closed her eyes as she turned to face the inn. And when she opened them, there was no one there but Joe. She wouldn't have minded a walk through the lane with Joe. But they could always do that another day.
"Who is he, Joe? Do you know?"
"Will thinks it's the innkeeper who set out from here almost a hundred years back, to ride over to Halworthy. He was never seen again and everyone thought that he must have been murdered out on the

moor. But it could be anyone Ellie. There's no end to the legends and superstitions that surround the moor. We've even had one handed down through our family, though no one knows how it started."

"What legend is that then, Joe?" she asked, feeling much better now that they were out of that field and in the little meadow again, close by to the inn.

"Well it's more of a superstition really. It's that old tree in the ghost's field. My great grandfather told his son that the family must never take it down. Even if it dies, we must leave it there to rot away. It seems that it's watched over our land for as long as anyone can remember, and the good fortune of any of the Allen family who still live in the farmhouse, will be lost forever, if its roots are dug up or disturbed.

"There's all manner of treasure hidden in those caves, Harry. Treasure stored away that weren't ever recovered. A few years back a bit of smuggling were a way to make life easier for folk. Goods brought in from a French cutter, waiting out off shore with kegs full of liquor and a bit off baccy. No harm done except to the Revenue. But it weren't always that way lad. Sometimes it were wicked. No other word for it. Honest vessels lured on to the rocks by cruel men, wrecked and plundered, good seamen drowned or murdered, and all for greed, Harry. Times best forgotten I say. But there are some things happened at sea that leave us to wonder lad, make for stories that become great legends. I think that pendant of yours came off a British ship, the Albermarle. She were blown ashore in a storm back in 1708, stranded on the rocks somewhere off Polperro and carrying a very precious cargo from foreign parts. Silk and indigo so they say, coffee and pepper, but that's not all, Harry lad, she were carrying diamonds. Most of the crew survived to tell the tale, but the ship were a total loss. The strangest thing happened after that though boy. The Albermarle completely disappeared, and most of her freight along with her. No wreckage from that good ship were ever found."

The old seaman reached out and took the pendant, along with its tarnished chain, from Harry's hand. "Bit of polish is all it needs. Bring it up good as new. Solid silver this is, and a fair sized moonstone if I'm not mistaken. Pretty stones, changing colour with the light, not what you'd call valuable though boy, not like the diamonds I reckon were stored away somewhere in those caves after the loss of the Albermarle."

Harry leaned back in his chair, watching old Giles Siddall puff slowly on his clay pipe, turning the pendant over and over in his weather beaten hand. He had hoped to find Giles there at the Jolly Sailor pub in Looe that evening, watching the boats come and go from his usual seat beside the small leaded window that overlooked the harbour. Harry had learned a great deal from him over the past two years, about the people who lived on the southern coast of Cornwall and earned their living from the sea.

"Surely any treasure from the Albermarle would have been discovered way back, Giles," he said. "1708? That's nigh on a hundred and seventy years gone by."

The old man held the pendant up between them, before placing it back in Harry's hand.
"To my mind you've the proof right here that there's more to be found yet in those caves. Search around close by to where you found your moonstone, Harry. I reckon it'll bring you luck."
"Well it does seem to bring me luck when I'm fishing for my supper off the rocks." Harry laughed and put the long chain around his neck, tucking the pendant inside his shirt and out of sight.
"Looks like your maid's back safe and sound." Giles tapped on the window, drawing Harry's attention to the small drift net boat being moored up alongside the inn, and the four young women standing around it.
"Brave women. All of them." Giles was saying, as Harry watched them secure the boat's moorings before leaving it for the day. "It takes courage to follow your husband's trade and support the family when he's dead and gone."

The women were walking away from the quayside, drifting off in different directions towards their homes, but the youngest was making her way across the little beach towards the inn.
"I don't know how you managed to land that little catch, Harry, but you've got yourself a good girl there."

“I’d like to think that she’ll be my girl one day, Mr Siddall, but right now she’s still grieving for her husband.”
“That’s as may be lad, only natural, but you’re more to her than a shoulder to cry on. You mark my words.”
“I’ll meet Mirrie outside,” Harry said, standing up to quickly finish his drink. “and I’ll let you know if I find anything more in the caves.”

Giles Siddall chuckled to himself as his young friend hurried off to meet Mirriam Thomas. She was known amongst the locals as ‘the little mermaid’, partly because of the work she had chosen for herself, and partly because she looked just like one of those ‘maidens of the sea’, with her long golden hair and lovely face. They had all mourned with her when her husband of less than two years had been lost out fishing the waters off Scilly, washed overboard in a storm, and leaving her with a small boy to raise on her own. But she wasn’t alone. There were too many young widows in the ports and coastal villages of Cornwall, scraping a living wherever they could, to care for the youngsters and elderly parents their men had left behind them. Mirrie’s husband had owned and skippered the boat that was moored outside, and when she’d finally accepted that he was never coming home again, she’d manned the boat that her dead husband’s crew had brought back to its home port, with her own crew of young widows. Giles took his cap off to them all. It was a dangerous and back-breaking way for women to make a living.

Harry realised that something was wrong as soon as he set eyes on Mirrie that evening, outside The Jolly Sailor. Instead of linking her arm through his to begin the long walk up to her cottage on the hillside above the quay, she turned away from him and sat herself down on the long wooden bench at the front of the inn.

"Something wrong?" he asked as he sat down beside her.

"No, Harry," she replied "but I do have something to tell you."

He had befriended her in the spring, not long before he'd left Cornwall to fish Scottish waters and quite soon after her husband had been lost at sea. She had been walking in rain and strong winds, her small son by her side, at the edge of the waves that had crashed on to the sands of Looe beach that day and flooded around their feet. He had called to her, encouraged her away from the water, and back up to the safety of the windswept beach and the little cave that had been his home for several days. She'd told him of the hours that she'd spent over the past few weeks searching in the coves around Looe and Polperro for her husband John Gilbert, who had gone overboard, and disappeared whilst fishing off the Islands of Scilly; the husband she was sure was still alive.

"He hasn't left us," she'd said. "He wouldn't leave me or our little Johnny."

Harry had known that he'd been only another shoulder to cry on, but since he'd returned to

Cornwall and found her much stronger, skippering her own boat with a crew of young women to fish local waters, he'd hoped that their friendship, which had grown out of sorrow, would one day blossom into a shared love, for he already loved Looe's 'little maid of the sea'.

"My brother-in-law came to see me at the cottage last night," she was saying. "He has found John. He came across him in a pub on Scilly and has taken his boat over there again today to bring him back to us."

Harry felt his heart twist and tighten in his chest.

"But why hasn't he come home to you before now?" he asked, seeing the nervous smile on Mirrie's face.

"He has been living with an old couple on the main island," she said. "John doesn't remember us. He didn't recognise his own brother. He has lost his memory, Harry."

"He will remember you when he sees you again, Mirrie. He will recognise his wife and son."

Harry took her hand in his, but she removed it gently.

"He is saying that he was saved from drowning by a mermaid. That she pulled him up from the bottom of the sea and swam with him to the shore. What will I do if he doesn't know us, Harry? Will he ever learn to love us again?"

"You were that mermaid, Mirrie. It was his love for you that saved him that day out at sea, and he will recognise you as soon as he sets eyes on you again."

"Thank you," she said. "I will never forget your kindness to me. I will never forget you Harry Reskelly."

Old Giles Siddall watched from the window of the inn as Mirrie slowly made her way towards the little path that would take her to her cottage. He needed no words from the lad to explain what he had witnessed. Harry's first love was walking away from him forever.

Ellie was always the first of her family to rise in the mornings. She had never been one to lie in her bed if she was awake, and so she had taken it upon herself to get the fires going downstairs and prepare the kitchen for any travellers who had stayed overnight at the inn. There had been no guests to fill their beds that night though, and so Ellie was surprised to find the fire in the bar dancing merrily on the hearth and someone asleep in old Bill Trenchard's favourite chair. There were two ways into the room; the one that she had used led away through the passageway, directly to the stairs, and the other entered the room from behind the bar counter.

As she didn't recognise the heavily booted pair of legs stretched out in front of the fireplace, she hastily backed out of the room and came in again through the second entrance, pausing just for a moment to pick up the loaded pistol that her father kept hidden below the counter. Nervously, she held the gun straight out in front of her as she approached the intruder again, this time face on. It was a young man, quite simply dressed apart from a fancy waistcoat; fast asleep in front of the warm fire that had all but died on the hearth the night before. He was handsome; dark skin glowing in the fire light; long coal black hair tied back from his strong face, to fall across his chest beside a silver set gemstone pendant.

"Harry Reskelly," she said softly. He started in the chair, opening his eyes, but otherwise staying very still.

"I appear to be at a disadvantage, young lady."

"I'm the innkeeper's daughter. Ellie Carter. How did you get in here? The doors are barred and bolted."

"I meant that I am not armed," he said. "If you'll put that gun down I'll explain."

She lowered the pistol in relief. He swung around in the chair but stayed there, watching the fire.

"I arrived in the middle of the night," he said. "I knew it would be warmer here than in my cottage."

"Joe says you always go to the farm when you first get back."

"Didn't want to wake them, so I thought I'd spend the night with my old lady." He smiled, looking around the room. "She hasn't changed."

"How did you get in here?" Ellie asked him.

He laughed, "Don't tell me Joe can't get in when the door is bolted. Any chance of breakfast?"

"Joe will be here soon," she said, leading the way to the kitchen, "you can eat together."

"And when do you eat, Ellie?" he asked, making himself comfortable at the table. "Do you have breakfast with Joe?"

"When we're not busy with guests," she said, "he's always up early to start in the stables."

"How long have you been living here, Ellie? When I left to go fishing in April, William Mason was the innkeeper."

"I heard he moved out in a hurry," she said. "His sheep had scab, but he allowed them to stray, and they infected old Squire Bray's flock. The Squire demanded compensation from him, but he refused to pay and disappeared overnight. We moved up here in May. My stepfather was working in Falmouth, in the docks, but he was a pub landlord in London before he came to Cornwall."

"You're not from London though, Ellie."

"I was born further down west," she said, "in Falmouth. Can't you tell? Joe used to laugh at my broad Cornish accent when we first met."

"I like it." Harry smiled at her. "It's gentle. Much softer than our North Cornwall accent. Do you miss your home?"

"I was lonely at first, but knowing Joe has changed that." Her eyes fell to look at Harry's pendant. "What stone is that?" she asked, tilting her head. "It changes colour as you move. It was glowing, amber and green, but now it's almost black."

Harry laughed, taking the pendant from around his neck and giving it to her.

"It's a moonstone," he said. "It reflects the changing light."

"It's beautiful!" She held it up towards the window. "Now it's blue," she said, "the purest blue. Has Joe seen it?"

"Joe, Joe, Joe." Harry's eyes were teasing her from across the table. "I can see I've been away too long. When's the wedding, Ellie?"
"He hasn't asked me yet," she said, still turning the pendant around in her hand and watching its colours change.
"But I can guess what your answer would be!"
"I love him," she replied, looking across at Harry, her face flushing a little.

"So you tell Reskelly first!" Joe was smiling as he looked in around the door.
"How did you get in?" she asked, giving the pendant back to Harry.
"Same way as this man I shouldn't wonder." Joe slapped his old friend on the back before sitting down beside him. "I had a feeling I'd find you up here this morning, Harry. Where have you been? We thought you were never coming home!"
"I came back to Cornwall early last month," Harry said. His face tightened a little and he avoided Joe's eyes. "I fell in love with a little mermaid, but her husband came back from the dead. After that … well I spent some time living on the beach, hunting for treasure in the caves, but I was missing the old lady, thought she might be pining for me … anyway, I'm here now and it's good to be home."
"So you weren't missing the rest of us then? Just the old lady …" Joe was teasing him now. Ellie watched them as she cooked their breakfast on the Cornish range. This man meant a lot to Joe. More than she meant to him? Harry looked up, his eyes studying

her face, looking into her own eyes as if he could read her thoughts.
"Ellie," he said, "sit down here with Joe. I'll finish the breakfast. We'll all eat together."
It was late that evening at Jamaica Inn when Eve Carter reluctantly announced that she was off to her bed.

"It's been good to finally put a face to your name, Harry Reskelly," she said as she stood beside him in the doorway of the bar. "And you've certainly improved our business tonight. It seems Robert Wilton is the only man who hasn't heard that you're back with us in Bolventor. He's been here at the inn two or three times a week since he returned to Palmer's Bridge to stay with his brother for the winter. Always asks after you. He brought his brother's little girl over to see us a few days back, riding up front of him on his brother's old horse. Sweet little thing she is."
"The little girl is Robert's daughter, Mrs Carter. His brother and sister-in-law look after her for him while he's away at sea, but she's Robert's daughter."
"The poor child's mother is dead then is she, Harry? They have lost her?"
"They've lost her all right, Mrs Carter, but from what I've heard she ran off with another man, three or four years back. Left Robert to bring his daughter up on his own. One of their neighbours saw her going off with this man in a carriage, and no sign of the baby girl. It seems that the neighbour had seen Robert go out earlier in the day, and so she took a look in their cottage and found the poor little girl all

alone and crying in her cot. Robert won't talk to anyone about it, but he's been a good friend to me. Watched my back out on the boats when I was younger. They don't come much better than Robert Wilton."

"Well I'm glad you told me about this, Harry, and I'll pass it on to Sam and Ellie, make sure they don't go asking Robert Wilton any unwelcomed questions. I'm sure he'll be in here looking for you tomorrow. It seems that you've been missed up here on the moor young man, although I heard my daughter didn't exactly welcome you home this morning."

Eve laughed. "I'm afraid I might be partly to blame for that, Harry. I was talking to Joe about ghosts you see, only a few days back, and Ellie overheard us. She thought such talk might frighten me, though she's never had any time for ghost stories herself, never believed in any of it. But the very next day, when Joe walked her down to the middle field behind the inn to meet a ghost, well something out there properly scared her. I'm sorry to say that she came back a firm believer in spirits, and not the kind that we have in those kegs behind the bar. What with that, and the highwayman who robbed poor Squire Bray a few days back, well I'm not surprised she had you looking down the barrel of a gun this morning."

"So, our highwayman has been up to his tricks again has he? We should all get together this winter and try to catch him out." Harry was looking around the room. Most of the local people who'd turned up at the inn throughout the evening had drifted away to their homes. Joe's father was still there though, drinking with Samuel Carter, and Ellie was with Joe

and his brothers, all of them standing or sitting around Bill Trenchard, and all close by to the fire.
"Joe did the right thing you know, Mrs Carter, taking Ellie across the old field. Not everyone's affected by the ghosts around Jamaica Inn, but if you are, then it's best you know something about them."
"You'd best tell that to Ellie then, Harry. Maybe it'll ease her mind. But we have a hunting party to feed and water in the morning, so I'll be away upstairs to get some sleep."
He bid her goodnight as she left the room and strolled over to lean against the wall beside the hearth. Sam Carter watched as Harry caught Joe's eye and quietly beckoned his friend over to the fireplace.
"Stay across in the cottage with me tonight Joe. I need to talk something over."
"Well as long as you don't keep me talking all night. We'll be busy here in the morning."
"I won't keep you up, but I need advice from someone I can trust. I can't sort this out safely on my own."

Sam's sharp ears had picked up every word.
'I can't sort this out safely.' It was likely that Harry would need better advice then Joe could offer him. If they would trust him, he would help them, but he didn't want them bringing trouble to his door.

Joe's family were the first ones to leave, and then Ellie, complaining because she would have to be up much earlier than was usual in the morning to help

prepare for the arrival of the hunting party. Bill Trenchard soon followed, struggling to his feet.
"It's time I was off to my bed as well gentlemen, or the wife won't be speaking to me in the morning. I'll walk over with you lads if you're ready."
"They can stay a while longer Bill if they've a mind to. I dare say it's warmer here than it'll be in Harry's cottage, and I've a few things to do outside before I bolt the door."
Sam left them in the bar together and followed Bill out of the inn. He watched the old man cross the road, to disappear into the little house next to Harry's, and then he returned; removing his boots to walk stealthily along the passageway that led into the room from behind the bar. They were facing towards him; huddled together at the counter and had no idea that he was there.

"How do you know they've not been stolen Harry, stashed away for a while until it's safe to collect them. If it were me I'd put them back before the thieves came after me. There must be plenty of people who know you're always down on the beach and living in those caves."
"I told you Joe, they're off a ship that was wrecked a couple of centuries back. No one knew they were hidden in those caves. Giles Siddall has his suspicions, but he doesn't know that I have these stones. I thought I might take them up to London. There's boats taking fish from Looe to London most days. If I just knew somebody on the dock. Somebody I could trust to tell me where I could find an honest diamond merchant."

“You’d never reach those merchants, my son. You’d be murdered for your diamonds before you left the docks. And who is this Giles Siddall?”

Harry jumped to his feet as Sam appeared in the doorway behind the bar. Several little stones scattered across the counter, shaken free from the pouch that he still clutched in his hand.

“Sit down lad. Your secret is safe with me. And I’m sure I can help you if you’ll trust me. But if you can’t put any faith in me Harry, then I’d advise you to do as Joe suggested and put your diamonds back where you found them. I can forget all about his little matter if that’s the way you want it.”

Harry sat in silence for several minutes before gathering up the scattered stones and then replacing them in their pouch.

“I’ll trust you Mr Carter,” he said. “I don’t want to lose my life over them. You know someone then do you? Someone who’ll give us a fair price and not turn us in to the Revenue.”
“If these diamonds were brought ashore from a shipwreck Harry, then there’s no doubt there will be those who’ll lay claim to them, however long ago they were lost. But you seem too have learnt a bit about them yourself. So before I do something that I’ll later come to regret, you’d better tell me what you know about this ship and her cargo, and more importantly lad, how much Mr Giles Siddall knows of the story.”

Harry reached back to lift the heavy silver chain from around his neck.
"It all started when I found this moonstone," he said, placing the pendant on the counter between them. I was searching about in a cave on Looe beach, about a month back. Thought I'd seen a bat in there. This was lying on a small ledge, quite high up ..."

"You know how to tell a good yarn, son," Sam remarked as the fascinating story of the unfortunate 'Albermarle' finally came to an end. "We'll be kept entertained on the stage coach to London with Harry for company, eh Joe?"
"Are we going to London together then, Mr Carter?" Joe's sleepy grey eyes were, for once, wide open.
"I was born in London's East End, ran a pub there for a while, but I fell foul of the law and had to leave in a hurry. Not that I'd done anything much myself, but I'd helped too many that had, if you know what I mean lads. There'll be a few of those men still there though who would see us right, man whose lives or liberty I saved in my time. And there's one man, if he's still around that is, who I know I could trust with my life, yours as well, if that's what it came to. I was a wanted man when I left London, and the City Police are still looking for me now. I may need the pair of you to watch my back so to speak. And if we delay going up until the cold weather sets in, I can keep my face covered on the streets without arousing suspicion."
"I can't ask you to do this, Mr Carter." Harry pocketed the pouch inside his coat. "You've made a good life for yourself here in Cornwall and there's

Eve and Ellie to think of. I can't ask you to risk getting arrested up there."
"You've not asked me to do anything Harry. I offered. And I brought it on myself, eavesdropping on you and Joe. Besides, I wouldn't mind seeing the old city again. Think on it lad, but don't worry on my account. I wouldn't carry those stones about with you though. We've a highwayman out there somewhere who seems to like haunting our old turnpike road."

The following day was the first Monday in November and a small hunting party was gathering outside of Jamaica Inn for the traditional start of the fox hunting season. Half a dozen men in scarlet coats, all wearing top hats or hunting caps and seated on fine horses, had already assembled in the yard before Squire Bray rode in to join them on a fine white hunter, accompanied by his pack of some thirty to forty excited hounds, already baying in anticipation of the forthcoming chase.

"No need to look quite so anxious, ladies." Squire Bray strode into the kitchen in search of Eve. "The Hunt has been meeting here over the winters for nigh on forty years. A hearty breakfast from your good selves, a tipple at your bar and we'll be on our way."
"Everything is ready for your party, Squire Bray. It's just that this is our first winter here. We're not used

to accommodating so many gentlemen on such an occasion."

"You soon will be, Mrs Carter. You soon will be, and I'll make sure you're well rewarded for your troubles. I'm very grateful you know, for your help the other evening. You've heard, I suppose, that a good friend of mine was accosted by the very same man two nights back? Took his purse, his high hat and his wedding ring. Whoever that scoundrel is Mrs Carter, he has no respect for the way a man might feel about his wedding ring. My friend should have been here today for this hunt, but he's too shaken up my dear lady, far too shaken up. Aah! Two more gentlemen to join us! I think that's all of us Mrs Carter. We're quite a small party today. I'll inform them that their breakfasts are ready."

At eleven o'clock that morning, Squire Bray, Master of the Hounds, sounded the hunting horn and rode away ahead of his pack, followed by the rest of his determined huntsmen. The few spectators that had turned out to watch them soon drifted away, leaving Eve and Ellie to clear and clean a sizable pile of dirty dishes and glasses.

With the work done in the kitchen Ellie called Joe and Harry in from the yard, where they'd been clearing up in readiness for the arrival of a stagecoach later that day.

"We've made a pot of tea," she said as they entered the kitchen. "I don't envy those horsemen today. It's looking grey and chilly out there on the moor."

"Don't waste your time worrying about them Ellie, they're all too fired up inside to feel the cold. Save your sympathy for Harry, he's walking down to Dozmary Pool later, to see if they'll take him on at the ice works again this winter."
"Have you seen the ghost of John Tregeagle, Harry?" Eve asked as they all sat down to the table. "I've been told that when he died he was condemned to empty the water in that pool every night, with a limpet shell."
"A limpet shell that had a hole in it!" Ellie shivered. "Poor man."
"He was a cruel man in life though Ellie, or so they say. I haven't seen his ghost as yet Mrs Carter, but who knows? Maybe he'll earn his salvation by helping us to harvest and store the ice when the pool freezes over. That would add a little more magic to the legends that surround Dozmary. But you've ghosts of your own, right here in the inn, that you need to know more about, if you are going to live peaceably alongside them. Has Joe told you about the ghost who haunts the east end of the loft, and passageway beneath it?"
"He hasn't," Eve said, "but since you seem to have your mind set on our knowing all about these poor souls, who haven't yet gone on to meet their maker, then maybe you should be the one to tell us, Harry."

Joe was grinning. "Harry's always been able to tell a good story," he said. "His grandmother taught him well. When she was a small girl her grandfather Tom was still alive, and she would sit at his feet and listen to his stories. He knew everything there was to know about the inn and the moor."

"This story starts in the November of 1777," Harry said, pouring himself a second cup of tea. "The following year of 1778 was to be the first time that the inn was improved, widened to join up with a new stable block and tack room. The same stables that we have here today. The original granite stonework was all covered in slate that year, to hide the alterations and help weatherproof the building. My great-great grandfather Tom had worked out here since 1750, when he'd helped to build the inn along with Jon Allen, who was Joe's great-great grandfather. Tom was living with Jon's family at Hele Farm back then, with his wife to be Ginny Rodda. Her husband had only been innkeeper here for about three months before he mysteriously disappeared one night in the autumn. Joe's told you about Ginny's husband, Jim Rodda, who was thought murdered out on the moor?"

"Will thinks it's Jim Rodda's ghost that haunts the field," Ellie said. "Do you think he's got that right, Harry?"

"He could well be right. I don't suppose we'll ever know for certain who it is. But with Jim Rodda gone, the inn needed a new keeper, and in the winter of 1777 a man by the name of Peter Kemble took over the tenancy, along with his wife Sarah. All apparently went well for the first few months after the Kemble's moved in. But in the early spring, a gang of seven or eight men arrived out here to start work on the improvements, and life began to go sadly wrong for poor Peter Kemble. It was said that his wife Sarah, a very attractive young woman, soon caught the eye of one of these men, and did very little to discourage him. This man was the son of a stonemason, who had set up a business from his own yard in Five Lanes using a local workforce of trained men to carry out building work, wherever they were needed, within a reasonable distance from their home town. Masons, carpenters, roof slaters and pavers, all used to working on chapels and coach houses, stables and barns. At first, these men, including the business owner's son, a carpenter by the name of George Grigg, all arrived for work each day in a horse and cart, and returned to their homes each night. But by the time that the work on the inn had come to an end, and the cottages were almost completed, winter was setting in. As the hours of daylight lessened each week, travelling across the moor in darkness, through mist and rain, with no shelter from chilling winds, was becoming increasingly difficult. The work had to be finished, and they decided to stay in the cottages overnight, and so get their job done, sooner rather than later. But what had begun as a little flirtation between George and Sarah, had, over the months, grown into a stronger relationship. Peter Kemble was often away from the inn for several hours at a time, visiting his older brother Phillip, who was also an innkeeper, at the King's Head at Five Lanes. Living across the road at the cottages, made it easier for George to take his affair with Sarah a step further, and it was common knowledge that he spent quite some time at the inn with her, whenever the coast was clear. Whether or not Peter Kemble ever suspected that there was something going on between them was never known, but one day, and hour or two after he had ridden away for Five Lanes, he returned to his home and caught the couple together, upstairs in one of the bedrooms. The two men fought, in the bedroom and outside of it, and all the way along the passage to the top of the back stairs, where Peter Kemble was pushed, from the top to the bottom, breaking his neck in the fall. He was dead, and George Grigg, fearing the hangman's noose for the murder, dragged his body up over the stairs and up into the loft, where he strung poor Peter Kemble up by the neck to hang from one of the beams, hoping that when his body was discovered, his death would be put down as suicide."

"But how was it discovered," Ellie asked, "that Peter Kemble had been murdered, pushed down the stairs to his death?"

"Sarah had seen it all," Harry replied. "She knew that her husband had not fallen to his death accidentally, and she knew as well that she could not keep that knowledge to herself. George left the inn, to return to the cottages and to his work, promising to come back to her one day when all of the upset over Peter's death had settled down. But as he left the inn by the main door, she fled out of the back and ran down over the fields to Hele Farm where she knew Tom and Jon were repairing a leak in the roof of the farmhouse. She told them everything, insisting that she wanted George brought to justice for the murder of her husband, even though they told her that she risked imprisonment herself for adultery or worse. It was Tom and Jon who cut Peter Kemble's body down and later stood as witnesses to Sarah's testimony at George Grigg's trial at the Assize Court held in the Friary Church in Bodmin. He was found guilty and condemned to a public hanging in the January of 1779. Sarah was never brought to trial and walked away a free woman, but she could not walk away from her dead husband and so she stayed on at the inn as the tenant, until her own death in the early 1800's. It's Peter Kemble who still haunts the east end of the inn today. His footsteps that can he heard on the back stairs and in the passageway beneath the loft. But it's said that he only appears if there is some kind of disturbance at the inn, the start of construction work, or a prolonged and heated argument."

"And knowing all of this is supposed to help us live alongside these ghosts is it then, Harry? Well I don't see it myself, not for the life of me." Eve stood up to stretch her legs and walk over to the kitchen window. "The mist has cleared," she said. "The pair of you had better finish your work clearing up that yard before the stage comes in."

"Will says that if you see a ghost, you should stay calm, bid them good day and …"

"That's enough, Joe Allen." Eve scolded him. "Go back to your work, and when you've seen to the stage, I suggest you both walk down to Dozmary Pool, blow some of those old cobwebs out of your heads. And take Mr Carter along with you, that is if you've a mind to find him."

"Where is he Mrs Carter?" Joe asked, "I haven't seen him since early this morning."

"Oh he's somewhere up in the loft," she said with a wry smile on her face, "over to the east side I think, repairing a bit of damage that's been done to one of the old beams."

Eve turned and winked at her daughter as the two young men hurried out of the room.

"We can all play at their little game, Ellie," she said.

"Don't you see enough water on those fishing trips of yours then lad?" Sam Carter asked, as the three men set out from Jamaica Inn to walk along the rough track to Dozmary Pool. "You'll have to work through the night to bring in ice thick enough to keep until summer. And how they can be so sure that it won't all melt away is beyond me! All your hard work could be wasted lad!"

"You'll understand when you see what's been done out here Mr Carter. The men have been cutting out a big chamber, similar to a cave in the hillside. It's lined with granite and the ice will be stacked inside and covered in turves of peat off the moor to preserve it. When I left here in the spring, we'd started to put in a drain below the chamber, so that any water can just run away, and the ice will stay dry."

"It's a lake, not a pool!" Sam exclaimed when he first set eyes on the waters at Dozmary.

"It's the source of the St Neot river, Mr Carter." Joe said. "We used to swim out here as boys."

"How deep would you say it is then?" Sam asked. "I've heard it said that there's no bottom to it."

"That's a myth, Mr Carter. You can walk right across it when we get a dry summer. It's deep enough now though. I wouldn't want to try walking through it today! Take Mr Carter over to look at the ice chamber, Joe. I'm going to the cottage to see if there's anyone about."

Sam and Joe were waiting at the water's edge when Harry finally emerged from the lone cottage that stood beside Dozmary Pool.

"There's half a dozen of them inside," he said, "having a bite to eat. And it seems they'll need all the help they can get once the ice forms and thickens up. The plan is to cut out blocks with chisels and saws and float it in to the land. There'll be a horse waiting to draw it up over a ramp and then take it to the chamber in the hillside."
"Well, pretty as the place is, I don't envy you lad. But you'll not need to work anywhere for a while if our little trip to London goes well. I've not told Eve that we're travelling up to the city together, so you'd both better be careful not to say anything to Ellie. They'll only worry if they're told too soon. Eve knows why I had to get out of London in a hurry, so she won't be too happy about it, but I'll tell her that I've a bit of business to sort out up there and that I'm taking you two along to watch my back. If we're lucky and my old friend is still living in the East End,
I'm hoping that we'll only be away from here for four or five days."

"Four or five days, Mr Carter? Surely the travelling alone will take the best part of that time."
"Not the way we're travelling, Joe lad. I've been looking into it for a day or two now, and it seems that the journey by steam train, Doublebois to Paddington London, will take about twelve hours!"

It was almost dark when Sam, Joe and Harry returned to Jamaica Inn together that afternoon. Ellie was waiting for them in the yard.
"The highwayman's around again," she said. "He robbed Luke Wonnacott and his passengers a couple of hours back. Luke stopped by here for a while before he took them back to their homes. The poor dears were all in need of a bit of comfort from us, and a hot cup of tea."
"We have to come up with a plan," Joe said. "Try to find out who this man is and stop him or it won't be long before innocent people will be too afraid to venture far from their homes, even in daylight."
"Luke could lose custom over this," Sam said. "Who's going to want to travel with him if they think they might be robbed by a highwayman?"

Luke Wonnacott was an enterprising young farmer's son from Altarnun, who like Joe, had little interest in farming. He had set up a passenger service, using his own small covered wagon and four horses, to carry people around on the moor, within a few miles from his home. There were farm houses scattered about between little hamlets and churches. Too far apart sometimes for the elderly inhabitants to walk or ride to visit their families, or to attend church or chapel.

Busy farmers were only too happy to allow Luke to ferry their wives and children to the little local food markets, or to the schools that had sprung up in some of the villages, and he sometimes changed his weary horses at Jamaica Inn if he was passing by after a long journey of seven or eight miles. Sam Carter owned the horses that were stabled in his yard, as the stage companies no longer supplied any horses to the inns that were used by their drivers. The railways had taken so much business from the roads that many stage coach routes had closed, and the companies were struggling, but in remote areas, where the railways had left gaps, stage coaches still held their own, and an innkeeper's horses now helped to boost the income he had lost due to the complete disappearance of the mail coaches, and the slow decline of the stage.

Fortunately for its tenants, Jamaica Inn, which stood on the edge of its own farm land, and was well known for letting its rooms to sportsmen in the winter, was still a thriving business.

"And did our man relieve anyone of their wedding ring today?" Harry asked.

"The widow woman who runs the little hardware store at Altarnun, and the pregnant farmer's wife from Five Lanes, both handed over their rings at gunpoint, and Luke's own grandfather gave up the silver cigarette case that he was carrying, a present from one of his sons, who was killed in a mining accident a few years back."

"It's bad enough that he takes their money," Sam said, "but it's the grief that comes with losing the

things that mean the most to you. That's what really upsets people."
"Well I don't see what we can do about it." Ellie pursed her lips. "Maybe we should call in the Constabulary from Bodmin. Let them look into it."
"We'll hold fire on that for while Ellie, see what we can come up with ourselves," Sam said, glancing quickly at Joe and Harry. "Ask your mother what she thinks of it, but I'm sure she'll agree with me!"

It was around eleven o'clock on the night before Christmas that Eve came into the bar, looking to have a quiet word with Sam. The little room was almost full with their 'regulars', all congregating together for a little Christmas cheer before making their way to Bolventor's Holy Trinity Church for midnight mass. Sam was over in the corner beside the fireplace, talking with Harry and Robert Wilton, and Eve quickly joined them.

"Parson Kellow is in the kitchen," she said, "asking if we'll bring a little donation down to the church tonight for the stain glass window."
"What makes him think we're coming to church tonight?" Sam asked her. "We'll have enough to do here Eve, clearing up after his gathering congregation!"
"Stop larking about, Sam. You know we're going to church tonight. But what am I to say to him about the money?"

“The Parson’s been raising money to replace that window for the best part of a year, ever since it were damaged in last winter’s storms. You’ve got to hand it to him though, he’s not shy to ask folk for their money.” Bill Trenchard had overheard their conversation, and stood up from his chair to join them.
“Send him in here Eve,” Sam said. “I’ll give him a generous donation before we go to the church. That should make our Parson happy. He may even spare us from the misery of a long sermon!”
“He’s called in here on his way back from a little trek around to some of the more remote farms and cottages,” Eve said. “He is very pleased with himself already, as far as I can see. Seems he’s collected quite a tidy sum from a few of the folk who can’t attend church tonight.”

As Parson Kellow readily accepted ‘a little Christmas tipple before church,’ and stood happily talking to Sam Carter, Harry left the room to look for Joe, and found him leaning against the wall at the bottom of the stairs.
“Where’s Ellie?” he asked.
“Gone to tidy herself up a bit before the service,” Joe said.
“She’ll be a while then. Walk over towards the church with me now Joe, before the Parson comes out for his horse. I’m thinking that we may well come across our highwayman out on the road tonight.”

Joe knew Harry too well to ask questions and hurried outside after him. It was a cold night, but the sky was clear; a near full moon lighting the way as they walked towards the gateway of the first field beside the road, not 500 yards from the inn.

"We won't be seen here," Harry said, sitting down close by to the hedge inside the entrance, and Joe joined him.
"Why would he come along here tonight Harry? Do you think him bold enough to hold up the congregation?"
"The Parson will be returning to the church ahead of his congregation, and according to Eve, he's carrying quite a bit of money tonight."
Several minutes had passed before the slow beat of a horse's hooves upon the road disturbed the silence of the night, and a horse and rider approached from the direction the inn.
"Stay down Joe and don't say a word, whoever it is. If it is our man, he'll be armed."

As they watched him, the rider reined in his horse beside the gateway and rummaged about in the pocket of his coat, before turning his horse to face the field, and then around to look back towards the inn. In the moonlight his face had been clearly visible. After pulling on a skull cap and mask he reached again for his pocket.
"Robert!" Harry jumped up to walk out in front of the startled horse. "You won't need that gun. Your secret is safe with me."

Robert Wilton's head dropped, and he froze in the saddle. "It's not loaded, Harry," he said. "The gun's not loaded."
"Well take off that cap and mask before the Parson comes along. Joe Allen is here with me. Come and sit with us for a while. Tell us what's possessed you to do this."

Robert dismounted, tethered up his horse and sat down with them, this time on top of the hedge.
"Why are you doing this, Robert?" Harry asked. "You earn good money on the boats in the summer, and you're living with your brother over the winter. Why in the name of God do you need to rob innocent folk of their money and their wedding rings?"
"My brother had his living taken from him when the turnpike trusts closed all the gates on the toll roads. He has to pay rent now to live in his house, and he's not a well man, Harry. Not well enough to take on work in the fields or come fishing with me. He needs easy work, but there's none of that around here. His wife does what she can, a bit of cleaning, a bit of washing, for those who can pay her, but she has her own little ones to look after, as well as my girl. I'm leaving this money that I take from people with my brother, to tide him over the summer while I'm away. I don't know what else I can do Harry."
"You can work over the winter, the same as I do," Harry said. "What's to stop you going back to Looe and fishing our local waters for a month or two?"

"My daughter's here Harry. She'll never know her mother, but she does still have her father, even if it is only for a few months of every year."
"Well she won't see much of you if you're locked away in a jail for the rest of your life Robert. How do you think she would feel about that, not to mention the shame of having a highwayman for a father?"
"Maybe Sam could sort your brother out with a few jobs around the inn. Serving behind the bar or giving me a hand. There's always work that I never get to finish." Joe stood up on the hedge, looking towards the inn.
"And you're coming down to Dozmary Pool with me to work Robert. They'll be working through the night there soon, bringing in the ice, so you'll have some free time to be with your daughter by day."
"Someone's coming down from the inn," Joe said. "I think it's the Parson."

"Well it's good to see a new face in our midst." Parson Kellow said, stopping his horse to speak with the three young men on the hedge.
"Robert's here to visit with family over Christmas, Parson Kellow," Joe said, jumping down onto the road. "He's a friend of mine Parson, a fisherman from Looe. A good Christian family man. He's coming over to the church with us, aren't you Robert? We were just waiting for you to come along."

Chapter Seven

February 1877

When Abraham Friedman heard the gentle knocking on the door of his little two up, two down terraced house in London's East End, he quietly crept up over the stairs, parting the curtains that covered his bedroom window, to look out onto the street. Three figures huddled together below him, in the darkness and the freezing fog, one of them knocking again on his door and then stepping back suddenly to look up at the window. Abraham darted out of sight, but the man had seen him and held up his arms, linking his hands together above his head; a signal that only his brothers used to let him know that it was safe to answer the door. But these men were not his brothers. Abraham parted the curtains again, scrubbed away a little of the thin film of ice that had formed on the glass and looked down again at the man who now stood motionless, still gazing up at him, whilst his companions rubbed their hands together and stamped their feet impatiently against the cold. It was Samuel Mason, he was quite sure of it now, the only man besides his brothers who had ever known and used his signal. He had not seen

Samuel in more than ten years and although he knew that he should not open his door, he also knew that he owed his life to this man and that he trusted him.

Joe and Harry eyed each other in surprise as the smallest man that they had ever seen opened his door to them on that icy winter's night. In the soft light that shone from the oil lamp on the table behind him, they could see that he was not much older than Sam, although his long dark beard was peppered with grey and his hair was almost white.
"Samuel Mason!" The man was exclaiming as he peered out at them from the partly opened doorway. "You are a sight for sore eyes dear old friend!"
"Then let your old friend in, Abraham, so that I can introduce you to my companions before we freeze to death out here on the street."

As the door opened a little wider, Joe and Harry dodged through the gap to follow Sam into a warm kitchen.
"Mason?" Harry mouthed, and Joe shrugged his shoulders before noticing that the little man was watching them.
"My friend here is Harry Reskelly," Joe said, holding out his hand to Abraham, "and I am Joe Allen."
With their introductions made, Abraham ushered them over to his table to sit in unexpectedly comfortable chairs.
"Shall I make you a hot drink, gentlemen?" he asked. "And I have fresh bread, butter and homemade jam?"

"That should warm us through very nicely my friend," Sam said. "We walked here tonight from Paddington Station as there were no carriages for hire on the street and we didn't wish to wait around, but we are chilled through to the bone."
"On a night like this the carriages are taken very quickly," Abraham said as he busied himself with finding them all something to eat. "But what has brought you back to London Samuel? I am very happy of course that you are here, and that you have chosen to visit with me, but I must admit to having resigned myself to never seeing you again."
"We came to London hoping to find you, Abraham, and I can't tell you how relieved I was to see you upstairs in your window, and to know that you are still alive and well. We have a little business to put your way, but before I explain you must bring me up to date with what's been happening around the old place. And I need you to tell me if your circumstances have changed at all, through the years that I have been away."

Abraham Friedman was, as Sam had explained to Joe and Harry before they left Cornwall, a Jew and a dwarf. His family had descended from a long line of diamond merchants, who had established themselves in a well to do area of London as far back as the early 1700's. Cutting fine stones to sell to the nobility they had earned themselves an unblemished reputation and were both well respected and extremely wealthy.

Abraham had known as much about diamonds as anyone in his family, but at the age of twenty-five, when he was already a wealthy man in his own right, he had tired of being so much in the public eye and of being treated differently to his brothers. And so he had chosen to live in the shadows of London's East End, faking poverty and for the most part shunning company. He had paid rent on a modest little house, furnished it sparingly but with comfort in mind and shopped for food frugally in the local markets. Any outward show of wealth would have been dangerous. He had attracted very little attention, made no friends, and was visited only by his brothers under cover of darkness. They had brought him money, which he could not spend, and little luxuries which he had kept hidden from the eyes of any prying passers-by, but this was the life that he had chosen for himself and for the most part, he had been happy.

The money that his brothers had brought him had accumulated over the years, and had anyone in the overcrowded and poverty stricken district known of its existence, then he would most surely have been robbed for it. As it was though, his money had remained his secret until the time that Samuel Mason saved his life, and nursed him back to health over days and weeks in his terraced house, which was situated close by to the pub where Sam was the landlord. Caring for Abraham in his bedroom, Sam had found money under his mattress. Cooking for him in his kitchen, he had discovered money hidden in tins in the larder, and behind a false panel beneath the sink. There had been bank notes placed into bags, which were nailed up under the seats of his chairs or placed under a few squeaky floor boards. Altogether it had added up to an enormous amount of cash, which Sam had admitted to finding, as soon as Abraham was up and about again. As a result of this he had been sworn to secrecy over his new friend's wealth and identity; secrets which he had never revealed to anyone right up to this very day, since all that even Joe and Harry knew of Abraham, was that he was a Jew and a dwarf, who would see Harry right with his diamonds, and could be trusted with all of their lives.

"So Samuel, you need to know if my circumstances have changed since you left the East End?" Abraham leapt up on to one of his chairs to sit at the table with his guests. "I grow a little older each day, a little more weary, but mostly I am content. My brothers continue to visit me, bring me little gifts, and sometimes I do wonder if I should rejoin them in the business, return to the life I was born to live, before my time on this earth has passed. I feel safe here though, a part of the scenery of these people's lives. No one notices me anymore. No one points or stares, except for the very small children from time to time, but that is to be expected. Have you told your friends here how you saved my life Samuel? That I would not be here today if it weren't for your bravery and kindness?"
"It was nothing. Anyone would have done the same if they'd been passing by that day."

"You were not the only person passing by, Samuel, but you were the only one who stopped to help me. I was set upon by three men one morning, on my way to the market," Abraham said, turning to look at Joe and Harry. "I could hear them approaching, though I could not see them, angry, drunken voices, complaining that they had been double-crossed by a street trader, a Jew. I turned back towards my home, hoping to step into a doorway before they caught up with me, but it was too late. They had a grievance with someone of my faith and, from the moment that they set eyes on me, they were going to punish me for it. As they came closer they were shouting, uttering profanities, but I kept my head down, kept walking, hoping that they would tire of their sport and pass me by. One of them though, caught me by the shoulder, pulled me back, and as I turned around, another of them knocked me to the ground, kicked me hard in the side and called out to his companions to follow suit, and put me out of my misery. I begged them for mercy, but that seemed to fuel their anger and they all set upon me, kicking me in the head and the chest until I could no longer feel the blows and began to slip away. They were circling around me, swearing, goading each other, intent I am sure on finishing me, when I heard a man shout out, cursing my attackers and calling them over to him to try their luck with someone of their own size. I heard the start of the fight that broke out, but the last thing I heard that day was a woman's voice in my ear. *'You'll be alright now dearie,'* she said to me. *'Sam Mason's here. Sam'll see to them and he'll look after you.'*

"It wasn't much of a fight, Abraham," Sam said. "They swung a couple of punches at me and then staggered off. They were all too drunk to do me any real damage."

"You saved me!" Abraham was determined that Sam's young companions should know the true story. "I woke up here in my own bed, with this man asleep in a chair at my bedside. He cared for me until I was well again and able to look after myself."

"You didn't know each other until that day?" Joe asked.

"Only by sight," Sam said. "We might have bid each other good day from time to time, but Abraham would never have set foot in my type of establishment. Isn't that right my friend?"

"Far too risky for me," Abraham chuckled, "but Sam looked out for everyone who needed his help, from defenceless little Jewish men to hardened East End criminals. Sadly it was to be his downfall."

"I was lucky, Abraham," Sam said, "landed on my feet. Life's good for me at the moment, but very little has changed around these parts from what I saw earlier out there on the streets."

"The people here are still stricken by poverty. Misery just breeds more misery. And yet they still dance on the street to the tune of a passing musician, or sing together in the pubs if they can spare the price of a beer. You young men might enjoy a drink in Sam's old pub. It changed hands a year or two back and the new landlord's encouraged a very different type of client through his doors. Music Hall artists mainly, and some famous faces from amongst the boxing fraternity."

"It's only a three minute walk from here lads," Sam said. "The Old Bell. Take a look over there in the morning if you've a mind to. I'll stay off the streets myself, but there's nothing to stop you two going out. We'll be moving on as soon as it's possible Abraham, but we're hoping to do a bit of business here before we leave."
"Business that you want to put my way, if I understood you earlier Samuel. What can I do for you my friend?"
"This is Harry's story, Abraham, and he does tell a very good story, but if you don't mind I'll close my eyes for a while in one of your comfortable chairs. The train journey was far more tiring than I thought it would be. I'm hoping that you won't mind putting us up in your house tonight my friend. I fear I might be recognised if we seek lodgings in any of the inns."
"You can all stay for as long as you wish," Abraham said. "I have a spare bedroom upstairs as you know Sam, and I can make up a bed or two of sorts down here by the fire."

As Sam got up from the table, Harry took out the shabby leather pouch containing the diamonds from the inside pocket of his coat, and gave it to Abraham.
"I am a fisherman, Mr Friedman," he said, "and I found these in a cave at the end of last summer. If they were stolen then I believe it was around one hundred and seventy years ago, when a ship named the Albermarle was wrecked off the Cornish coast and her cargo was plundered."

"The Albermarle!" Abraham exclaimed, shaking all of the glittering little stones out onto his table. "Why my boy, if you are correct then these little treasures are a part of the lost Friedman diamonds, a shipment, needless to say much larger than this, which was destined for London and the newly established Friedman Diamond Merchants. These would have been amongst the first shipments ever received by my family in this country. But they were stolen, as you said, plundered from the wrecked Albermarle which then mysteriously disappeared from the rocks off Polperro, where she had been stranded in a storm."
"You know the story, Mr Friedman!" Both Harry and Joe were staring at Abraham in astonishment. "Does this mean that these diamonds belong to you, to your family?"
"I was a diamond merchant my boy. It goes without saying that I would know the history of my family's business. But we didn't received the shipment, so therefore no money would have changed hands. If these little stones belonged to anyone, it would be to whichever company shipped them over to England all those years ago. I am sure that we have those records stored away somewhere. You could return them maybe, or my brothers may still wish to purchase them from whoever owns them."

Harry's face had fallen, and Abraham started to chuckle, slapping the table so that a few of the diamonds bounced and rolled towards the edge. Joe reached out to catch them, and scooped them all

back together in a pile. Abraham was still chuckling, a broad grin spread across his heavily bearded face.
"I am jesting," he said. "Part of the diamond shipment from the Albermarle was on its way to London, and to the forerunners of my family's business, but we have no proof as to how, or even when, these particular stones came to be left in a Cornish cave. I suspect that they were taken from a box of diamonds which had, at some time, been plundered from a shipwreck, hidden in the cave and eventually smuggled out of the county. These are someone's little nest egg, Harry, but the thief who stole from thieves failed to return for them, and so now they belong to you. Are you wanting me to simply put a price on them for you or to take them off your hands? My brothers would be delighted to own them, and have such a fascinating story to tell at their dinner table."
"I will be sorry to part with them, Mr Friedman," Harry said, "but I think it's time that they saw the light of day. They should be admired for what they are, not hidden in the shadows."

For a short while Abraham seemed lost in his own thoughts, his eyes fixed on the little pile of stones on the table. When he looked up it was to smile at Harry.
"You have a wise head on your shoulders my boy," he said. "A very wise head for such a young man. I will be more than happy to buy these stones."

He slapped the table again; far more gently than before. “I will need a little time though to examine them closely, put a fair price on them for you.”
“Tomorrow will do for that,” Sam said, getting up from his chair by the fire. “I’ll help you with our beds Abraham, and we’ll turn in for the night if that’s alright with you, catch up some more in the morning while these two take a look around the East End.”
“What d’you think they’re worth Harry?” Joe whispered as they both settled down in their makeshift beds.
“I wouldn’t like to say. Enough I hope to set all three of us up for a while.”
“I’ll not take a penny from you. It’s Sam that’s helped you and put his liberty on the line. I’ve done nothing but come along as backup.”
“If you won’t take anything Joe, then I’ll put it aside for you. It’ll be yours to use, or to leave one day to your family, to your children!”

Joe lingered on the streets of the East End the next morning, shocked by the hunger on the children’s faces as they trailed behind him, intent no doubt on picking his pockets.
“Keep moving, Joe,” Harry urged him, coming back for the third time to look for his friend. “Keep up with me or they’ll soon rob you of your money!”
But Joe fell back from him again, halted by the sight of an old beggar woman, sitting huddled in the entrance of a small theatre with what appeared to be a baby in her arms. He approached her, and threw

some coins into the wooden box which lay by her side.
"Have you nowhere warmer to take your grandchild?" he asked, as she opened her eyes to look up at him. A faint smile flickered across her face before she closed her eyes again.
"I'm lookin' after 'im," she croaked, "for 'is muvver. I 'ave no 'ome to take 'im to."
"Come away. She does this every day. She'll be alright," Harry said, catching Joe by the arm. He had seen poverty like this in the cities up north and knew that there was nothing they could do to help her. He turned away but Joe pulled him back.
"Harry wait! Look at that!" He was pointing at a billboard propped up outside the theatre doors behind the old woman. On the billboard was a poster, and on that the portrait of a young woman, and the words

FLORRIE RESKELLY
APPEARING HERE ALL WEEK IN
'EAST LYNNE'

"It won't be her, Joe. Not my sister Florrie."
"Why not?"
"Not here in London. Not an actress."
"You don't know where your family went Harry. Or what any of them are doing. And she's about the right age."
"There will be a lot of women with that name. All over the country. I'm telling you it's not her."
"Well, since we're here, there's no harm in trying to find out," Joe said, and leaving Harry to stare after

him, he walked in through the doors of the Albion Theatre and straight up to the ticket booth in the foyer.
"What can I do for you then, dearie? A ticket or two for tonight's performance?"

A stout little woman with orange hair was smiling out at him, hopefully pawing the pile of tickets on the counter in front of her.
"Maybe," Joe said. "If we're around tonight. I was wondering though if Miss Reskelly is in the theatre now. If we could speak with her. My friend's just outside on the street you see, and I think she could be his sister."
"His sister! Well that's a new one on me. Not bad though. Not bad at all. But no one gets in to see Florrie, dearie. Not without 'er 'usbands say so."
"Her husband. So Reskelly is her husband's name? Her married name?"
"These girls are always changing their names, dearie. They'll change their name like they change their clothes if it'll bring them a bit more fame and fortune. But Florrie's kept to 'er own name as far as I know, and I've known 'er a few years now. She came up through music hall with the name of Florrie Reskelly. Good she was too. Voice like a bird. But when Dave Grimes took over this theatre, well he took over our Florrie with it, if you know what I mean. Married 'er. Kept it respectable, but she weren't allowed to do music hall again. No more singing and dancing for Florrie. She's an actress now, and a fine one at that. And she wouldn't change her name on the billboards. Said Florrie

Reskelly sounded better than Florrie Grimes! But I don't think our Mr Grimes would want Florrie entertaining any young men backstage though dearie, brother or no brother."
"So she is in the theatre," Joe said. "Do you think she would come out to the foyer to talk for a few minutes?"
"I am here already sir. I came out to talk to Annie, and I'm afraid I've been eavesdropping on your conversation from behind the foyer curtains."

Joe turned as a smiling young woman stepped out of the shadows behind him.

"We haven't been introduced," she said, holding out her hand, "but since you claim to know my brother, I am far too curious to worry about little formalities. I'm Florrie Grimes. Reskelly was my maiden name."
Joe took her hand. "Joe Allen," he said. "I want to ask you so many questions, but it's Harry you should talk to. Will you see him?"
She laughed. "Since it's Joe Allen who is asking, then I must! But I will see him before I talk to him," she said, and still holding Joe's hand she led him to the theatre doors and peered through a glass pane at the street outside. "I see him," she said, watching Harry as he stood huddled up in the entrance close by to the old beggar woman. "Bolventor would not have been dull, with you two for company! You must bring him in from the cold."
She turned back to Joe and released his hand, her dark eyes full of mischief. "I have heard all about you from my mother."

Harry looked so awkward when he came in through the doors, that Florrie held out both her hands to him.
"Harry," she said. "Our grandmother called you Reskelly then, not Polkinghorne?"
"She said it suited him better." Joe answered for Harry, since he took his sister's hands but didn't reply.
"We'll talk in the end dressing room, Annie," Florrie said, turning to the astonished little woman in the ticket office. "It's the nearest to the back entrance. Let me know if anyone comes in."
"Don't you mean if your 'usband comes in?" Annie muttered, her eyes fixed on Harry.
"Anyone, Annie, I said anyone!"

She sat them down on little chairs in a room cluttered with costumes and makeup. *It all smells as lovely as she looks, Harry thought, admiring her pretty face.*
"Seems like a good way to make a living," he said, glancing around at a stack of hats and wigs on a long bench.
"Better than most," Florrie said. "What do you do for a living, Harry? Why are you here in London?"
"We're here on a little business with Joe's future father-in-law." Harry grinned at his friend. "I'm a fisherman in the summer months Florrie, but I work around Bolventor in the winter."
"So Joe Allen's got a girl. I know all about your family Joe, the Allen family, and their connection to the Trelawny's. That you were born at Jamaica Inn just six months before Harry. Our mother told us

girls endless stories about Bolventor after our father died. She was happy there."
"He's gone then," Harry said. "Where did he take you all, Florrie? Where did you go after I was born?"
"We travelled into Devon, to Plymouth, and he found work as a fisherman for a while, sometimes bringing the catches up to London. That's when he decided to move us all up to the East End so that he could earn better money, working in the docks. Mother used to say that he had always worked hard. He was killed there when I was seven. Some sort of accident. I don't remember him that well, Harry."
"And our mother?" he asked. "Is she alive?"
"No, Harry. Sadly we lost her ten years later, when I had just turned seventeen. She almost died of grief when our father was killed. She loved him Harry, couldn't imagine life without him. That's why she took us and left you with our grandmother on the night you were born. She knew you'd be safe with her mother, and with Joe's family around to lend a hand. She never forgave herself though."
"Why didn't she come back to her home after he was killed, Florrie? Grandmother would have forgiven her."
"I think she was too ashamed. Couldn't face everybody after walking out on you and taking three granddaughters away from her widowed mother. She was working before he died, cleaning for a few hours every day in the 'Old Mo', the music hall in Drury Lane. But the money wasn't enough to feed us and pay the rent man. We would have been thrown out onto the streets before too long, if one of

the owners hadn't heard her singing while she went about her work. He gave her a chance to perform on the stage and the audience loved her. She was only thirty when our father was killed, Harry, and still a 'real looker'. She became quite a star around here and earned enough money to keep a roof over our heads and buy us pretty dresses. The best part of it for me was being allowed to stay backstage in the 'Old Mo' whenever she was working."

Florrie paused, her eyes searching Harry's face. "I can see something of her in you," she said.

"How did she pass away?" he asked and Florrie sighed.

"It wasn't a good way to die," she said. "She was about to go on stage when a fight broke out between two of the stage hands. I was there that night but I never found out what it was about. It was the worst fight that I had ever seen. It was as if they truly hated each other, and mother must have thought that she could stop them by stepping between them, reasoning with them, but at the moment that she stepped in, one of them pulled out a knife, a knife that he always carried for his work. It was our mother that fell, Harry, stabbed in the chest and dead within a few minutes. I held her while she died and she only spoke one word, *"Daniel"*. That's how much she loved him. Our father was the only one she called for as she passed away."

"Somehow it helps to know that," Harry said. "I don't understand why it helps, but I do feel that I know her a little now, know why she did what she did."

"Miss Florrie! Miss Florrie!" Annie was knocking on the dressing room door, pushing her head in around as she opened it. "I've been watching outside Miss Florrie, and Mr Grimes is coming along the street right now!"

"Then I'm afraid we'll have to part company far too soon," Florrie said as she stood up to join Annie in the doorway. "I'll show you to the back entrance. See if you can delay my husband for a moment or two Annie."

She hugged and kissed them both before they left her, holding on to Harry for as long as she dared.

"My sisters?" he asked urgently as she tore herself away from him. "How are my sisters?"

"Alive and well, brother," she said. "Both married and happy. Don't worry about us. Don't worry about me. I do wish we could have all grown up together, but it wasn't to be and I am very happy here now with my Mr Grimes."

The door at the rear entrance to the Albion Theatre opened out onto a grubby cobbled courtyard, almost entirely surrounded by tall terraced houses with small unwashed windows and sloping wooden balconies. Three small children watched Joe and Harry from beside their mother whilst she hung shabby little clothes out to dry over the railings. A woman's pale and haunted face looked out at them from behind a broken window pane.

Harry shivered and slapped Joe on the back. "Let's get out of here. I think we need a stiff drink at The Old Bell."

Harry hardly spoke a word as they walked away from The Albion Theatre and his youngest sister Florrie. Sensing Harry's need for some time to himself, Joe stayed silent, pacing along beside his friend until they reached the pub where Sam had once been the landlord. Passing through a wide archway between a baker's shop and a bacon drying business, they found themselves facing the front entrance.

"Looks as if it's not long been done up," Joe said, as they passed through freshly painted little double doors.

"To encourage a very different type of client," Harry replied, quoting Abraham. "I wonder how we'll fit in?"

They ordered whiskies and Harry paid, though Joe was searching around in his coat for his money.

"I owe you a debt I can never repay, Joe," Harry said as they sat down with their drinks at a table in a dark corner of the room. "You can at least accept a whisky from me."

"It seems I have no choice," Joe grumbled, pulling out the linings of his pockets. "I've had my pockets picked!"

Harry's tense mood soon faded away in the friendly atmosphere of the recently modernised East End pub. Shiny polished tiles and glass had replaced much of the old wood, so that it looked bright and spacious. It was quiet, only six other customers besides themselves. On the far side of the room four ladies sat together, and although it was still only mid-morning, all of them were dressed elaborately in what looked very like stage costumes. Perched on stools at the bar, two middle aged men were engaged in a lively conversation. Whilst one was dressed in a silk shirt, bow tie, waistcoat and white trousers, the other, a Scotsman, wore a fitted coat, a red white and black kilt, and the heavy socks of another tartan.

"Sam would scarcely know the place," Joe said. "It's a great shame he can't come along and take a quick look at it. Though I would have quite liked to …" Harry interrupted him.

"Seriously Joe, without you I wouldn't have met my sister today. It's been something I've dreamt about for as long as I can remember, finding out what happened to my family. Maybe meeting up with them one day and yet, even if I had noticed that poster myself, I would have just walked on by."

"Don't forget that I sat and listened to your grandmother's stories with you Harry. I wanted a happy ending to them, probably as much as you did. But there is pain in the ending, as well as pleasure. It was hard finding out what happened to your parents."

"Not the best of ways to die, as Florrie said, but at least I do know what happened to them now, and my sisters. And Florrie's strong, a survivor like my grandmother. She reminded me of her, so sensible and kind."

Hearing loud cheers and laughter from the far side of the room, Harry looked up to see a blowsy young woman in a low cut dress swaying across the room towards them.
"What's so serious that it's keepin' you from your liquor, my lovelies," she shrilled, as she came closer to them, pointing to their drinks on the table. "You 'aven't touched a drop! Come with me and sit with us ladies. We'll soon put smiles on those 'andsome faces of yours!"

The ladies beckoned, leering smiles on painted lips inviting them to their doom. Joe paled as his friend stood up, lifting his glass from the table.
"I am sorry to disappoint you ladies," Harry said, raising the glass and swallowing its contents. "But my companion here has had his pockets picked, and this is the only drink we had the money for today."
The blowsy young woman put her hands on her hips and turned away to march back across the room. The ladies had already lost interest in them and Harry sat down again.
"Drink up, Joe," he said. "We should get back to Sam. I've a feeling he'll want to leave London tonight."
"But what about your money?" Joe whispered. "Surely Abraham will have to get that from his brothers before we can leave?"
"Sam wanted us out of the way this morning Joe. I'm sure those two will have arranged something between them by the time we get back."

A smiling Abraham opened his door before they had time to knock.
"We have been watching out for you," he said as they came in from the cold. "I have been to the market for pies and fresh fruit. Sit and talk with Sam. He is eager for news of The Old Bell."

As they sat by the fire, telling Sam of their meeting with Florrie, Abraham brought food and hot drinks to the table.
"We'll eat together," he said, "before you catch the train back to Cornwall."
"Are we to leave today then?" Joe asked. "I was hoping for some time in the West End of London while Harry showed the diamonds to your brothers, Mr Friedman."
"Sam cannot wait for that, young man," Abraham said. "He needs to leave London before someone recognises him. I have put a price on the diamonds for you Harry, and I will buy them from you myself if you still want to part with them. I had no trouble collecting the money this morning." He laughed at the incredulous expression on Joe's face. "We do have banks in the East End of London my boy," he said.

With their meal over, Sam and Joe left Harry at the table with Abraham to count the money.
"I overheard you talking with Joe last night," Abraham said in a low voice, "and I'm trusting you to keep your word and give my friend Samuel a fair share of the money. I have been generous to allow for this, as I see it as the only way that I can repay

him, at least in part, for saving my life. He would not take it you see if he thought that I had given you extra money that was a gift for his kindness to me. He is a stubborn man."

"What if he won't accept anything from me Mr Friedman? Joe is already refusing to take a penny of the money."

"Then tell him that you will put the money aside for him Harry, for him or for his wife and daughter. I am trusting you to do exactly the same for Samuel as you will do for your friend."

"You have my word, Mr Friedman," Harry said. "The money will be divided fairly."

As Sam, Joe and Harry walked through the streets of the East End that evening, on their way to Paddington Station, Abraham sat alone once more at the table in the kitchen of his little terraced house. He took the leather pouch from the pocket of his coat and shook out the diamonds to examine them again. They were valuable, there was no doubt about that, but they would not fetch anything close to the amount of money that he had given to Harry Reskelly. Released from the shadows though, the diamonds had freed him from several burdens. He had always hoped that he would one day be able to do something for Samuel in return for his help, and the diamonds had given him that opportunity. He was also glad to be free of the money that he had accumulated in his house over a quarter of a century. He should have told his brothers at the outset, not to bring him money that he could not spend; money that he could not safely possess. The diamonds had relieved him of that burden and his brothers would repay at least a part of his money in return for the precious stones once plundered from the Albarmarle. He would ask them to bank most of it for him; put just a little away for his use, in the safe that he planned to have installed in his new home in London's West End. He was going home; re-joining his brothers in the family business as they had so often begged him to do. Spending time in Sam's company again, and in the company of the two polite and friendly young men that Sam had brought with him from Cornwall, had made Abraham realise that not only had he been lonely for far too long, but also that most of the people that he had met in his life had respected and admired him for his knowledge and achievements. If he had been treated differently to his brothers, it was because he was different. It had been Harry's words though that had put it all together for him, *'It's time that they saw the light of day. They should be admired for what they are, not hidden in the shadows.'*

To Abraham the little diamonds were priceless. They had freed him from his burdens and he was going home.

Chapter Eight

Spring 1877

In early March, Parson Kellow was delighted to receive an anonymous donation towards the stained glass window in Bolventor's Holy Trinity Church; the window that had been damaged fourteen months earlier in the storm. This money, along with his earlier collections, enabled him to replace the window well before Joe and Ellie's wedding in mid-April.

As the bells rang out to announce their union, the couple were married in a church filled with flowers, surrounded by family and friends. After the ceremony they were greeted outside the church by a cheering cluster of villagers; smiling men and women wearing their Sunday best; young boys dressed in freshly washed smocks; small children sitting in wheeled, wooden carts, and the Parson, standing beside the parish clerk. Small girls, all dressed in white, gathered together to walk ahead of the bride and to scatter petals, herbs and seeds in her path. Joe and Ellie's well-wishers formed a procession behind the wedding party, to shout their congratulations all the way back across the fields to Jamaica Inn.

Ellie's white wedding gown and bonnet had been made for her by a dressmaker in Launceston. Her small flower bouquet was tied with blue ribbons, and around her neck she wore Harry's moonstone pendant.

'I'll need something old to wear on the wedding day Harry,' she'd told him, eying the pendant one morning as they sat together, waiting for Joe to arrive for breakfast.

'And why is that?' he'd asked, smiling as he covered the pendant with his hand.

'It's an ancient custom, wearing certain things that have been chosen to bring good luck. Every bride should wear something new; that will be my dress, something blue; I already have blue ribbons, something borrowed; I will have to borrow a handkerchief from mother, something old; I do so want to wear your moonstone, Harry. You know how much I admire it.'

He'd laughed, standing up to place the pendant around her neck. 'Then you must wear it on your wedding day, Ellie,' he'd said. 'But it will have to be your 'something borrowed'. I don't want to discover that the bride has to keep her 'something old' in order to keep her good luck!'

He had placed it around her neck again on the morning of the wedding. 'This will be yours one day Ellie,' he'd said. 'I promise you. It has brought me good luck but I can't let you keep it right now. I still need it.'

As the wedding party filled the downstairs rooms of the inn, Eve brought out a rich wedding cake, decorated with frostings of orange blossoms, and the food that Ellie had helped her to prepare for everyone who could stay on for a while after the ceremony. Joe, looking happy but awkward in his smart suit; a ruffled cravat about his neck, helped Sam to serve everyone with a drink.

Bill Trenchard's favourite chair had been moved away from its usual position in the centre of the room, over to the corner beside the bar, facing out towards the door.
"This'll do me for today," he said, settling down with his ale and his pipe. "I'll need it moved back again tomorrow though lads. You know I like to sit and watch the fire."
"We thought you'd be better off over here Bill," Joe said, grinning at Harry. "You'll be first in the queue for your refill without getting up from your chair!"
"Well there's something in that I suppose. Fair tuckered me out it has today, walking down to the church and back. Wouldn't have missed it though, not for the world. And my missus, God rest her soul, would have been proud of you Joe, marrying a lovely girl like Ellie." He fell silent, tears in his eyes as he puffed on his pipe, turning his head away to watch the door.

"Congratulations Joe. I hope everything will work out for you." Robert Wilton joined them at the bar and briefly shook Joe's hand.
"We thought we'd see you at the church," Harry said. "What kept you away?"
"I …er…couldn't get there … something I had to do …sorry Joe. I was hoping for a quick word with you though Harry, if you could spare me a few minutes."
"We'll talk over by the fire then Robert," Harry said quietly, catching his friend by the shoulder and steering him away from the bar. "The Squire's just walked in and I don't want him coming face to face with his highwayman. Joe tells me that he got quite a good look at you that day Robert."

"I've been told the bridegroom is in here!" Young Squire Bray strode into the room and up to the bar to shake Joe's hand. "Congratulations young man! I wish you a long and happy marriage! I've only been married for seven months myself, as you know, but I can thoroughly recommend it! Now where is the blushing bride? A man should be with his wife on their special day, not serving drinks to his wedding party!"
"Good day to you, Squire." Sam came into the room through the door behind the bar, carrying a barrel of ale. "The Squires right, Joe. You should be with Ellie. I can manage here. Now, what can I do for you, Squire?"
"Well I won't say no to a brandy," the young Squire said, as Joe left the room to look for his bride. "and I was hoping to speak with your lady wife. I have a bit of business to put your way."

"She'll be in the kitchen Squire, if you want a word with her."
"No, no. She'll be busy. I wasn't thinking. I want to arrange for my cousin to stay here. It's not until mid-September. Plenty of time. Family get-together. My, and my dear wife's, wedding anniversary and the old Squire's sixtieth birthday. The manor house will be bursting at the seams! Between you and me though, my cousin's a bit of an odd one, not much love lost between him and the rest of mankind. Doesn't trust people you see. Prefers his dogs and his horses. Won't have live-in servants. Won't put his money in a bank. God only knows where he keeps it! Carries quite a lot of it around with him, I do know that. Foolish man my cousin. But I thought he might be happier staying here for a few days. Not so many people around him. Breakfast in his room. Carriage to and from the house in the evenings. That sort of thing. What do you think, Mr Carter?"
"Oh, I'm sure that will be no trouble at all, Squire. And Mrs Carter can have a word with you a bit nearer to the date."
"September 14th Mr Carter, that's the date. The date my father was born and the date my wife and I were married. A day or two either side of that should set him up very nicely!"

"I'll be leaving soon," Harry told Joe a few days later, at the end of April, as they sat on the stile in the hedge behind the stables; looking out across the fields towards Hele Farm. "The boats will be sailing

up to Scotland next month, and Robert wants us to go out together again."
"How can you leave all of this every year?" Joe asked him. "Your friends, your home, the moors? It's not as if you need the money, Harry. There's enough in the bank account in Bodmin to keep you grounded for years to come. There's no reason for you to risk your life fishing out in the North Sea every summer."
"The sea is in my blood, Joe. I miss it when I'm here, in the same way that I miss you and the inn and the moors when I'm away."

Abraham had asked Harry to put aside a certain amount of money for Sam, and that he had done, in a bank account opened in Sam's name in Bodmin. To his relief, Sam had already used a little of the money, for the donation to the church towards the stained glass window.

Since Joe had refused to take any of the money that Harry had received in exchange for his diamonds, Harry had opened a joint bank account, in both his own and Joe's names.
'I won't use the money,' Joe had insisted, shocked to learn that Harry had also paid a visit to Peter & Peter, the solicitors in Launceston, and made a will, leaving him everything that he owned, including his cottage.

'Why are you leaving it to me?' Joe had asked him. *'You have three sisters, and we can contact them*

through the Albion Theatre. This doesn't feel right Harry!'

'My grandmother would turn in her grave if I left the cottage to anyone but you Joe. You know how she felt about it! And if I come to an untimely end out at sea, I want you to have the use of my money. This way there will be no dispute about the cottage, and I will die with complete peace of mind.'

They had said no more about it until this moment, but Joe had been pondering over ways to keep his friend from going out on the long fishing trips every summer.

"Well I don't want you drowning in Scottish or Irish waters," he said. "You could fish in our local waters Harry, or sail as far as London, take the fish to Billingsgate Market. That way you could see Florrie from time to time."

"I don't want to spend too much time in Looe now Joe," Harry said. "Mirrie's husband will be there, and they will have all settled down again together as a family by now. I would like to pay old Giles Siddall a visit though, make sure Mirrie's happy before I set sail for Scotland. I need to find a woman of my own Joe, and I won't find her working around here or down at Dozmary Pool."

"And you won't find her out in the middle of the North Sea, Harry," Joe grumbled. "Not unless she's a real mermaid."

Squire James Ridge from Southwick in Wilshire, arrived in the evening of September 13th 1877, at

Jamaica Inn, in the private carriage which had, as arranged previously by young Squire Bray, picked him up from the railway station at Doublebois, and brought him north across the county and then across the moors to Bolventor. He was, Ellie thought, quite a handsome man, in a dark dishevelled way, and not quite the recluse that Squire Bray had made him out to be.

"It's a great pity that my cousin didn't think to suggest that I stayed here last year, my dear," he said, as Ellie took him up to the room he was to occupy for the next two nights. "This is far more suitable for me. Quiet, secluded accommodation … very tidy and clean it is too, my dear," he added as she opened the door. "It's my hearing you see, not quite what it should be I'm afraid. Too many people, all chattering away around me and I can't make out a word that they are saying."

"Squire Bray made all the arrangments for your stay with my mother," Ellie said. "She was asking if you would prefer to have breakfast in your room?"

"Spendid idea. Seven thirty. Bacon, eggs, mushrooms if you have them. But no black pudding. Not to my taste, black pudding. And I won't be down again tonight, my dear. I am planning to take a walk on the moor in the morning. My cousin is sending a carriage for me in the evening, just before sunset."

Eve and Ellie watched in the morning as Squire Ridge set out for his walk on the moor. It was a fine dry day, but nevertheless Eve warned him to stay on the beaten tracks, and to keep well away from the marshlands and spongy wet bogs.

"Have no fear dear lady," he told her. "I will take great care. Ending my days in a Cornish bog holds little appeal for me."

To everyone's relief, he reappeared in the middle of the afternoon, looking even more dishevelled than he had the night before. Joe and Ellie were sitting outside in the sunshine as he limped through the entrance and into the yard.
"Strained a muscle," he explained, stopping for a while beside them to flex his left leg. "I took Mrs Carter's advice and stayed on the paths, but I have to say that I soon lost my way. Each of those little tracks looks very much the same as the next. I turned this way and that, thinking I would never find my way to the inn."
"You were fortunate to find your way back." Joe said, standing up to let Squire Ridge sit down beside Ellie.
"Well, as it happens, I hadn't strayed too far away," the Squire said. "A twenty minute walk, no more. I was indeed fortunate. Very fortunate as it happened, to meet a young man on the road who was heading in this direction. I asked him the way to Jamaica Inn and he smiled, bade me follow him and walked on so quickly that I hurt my leg in the effort to stay close up behind him. He didn't turn or speak to me again until we came so close to the inn that I could see the chimneys and the roof against the skyline. Only then did he turn to wish me well, and to leave me, taking a little road to the right that led back onto the moor. I was so surprised that it didn't cross my mind to thank him."

"He took the road to Dozmary Pool," Joe said. "We'll thank him for you Squire, if we see him."
"But how will we know him?" Ellie asked.
"You'll know him if you see him my dear. There can't be many like him around these parts. Good looking young man. Strongly built. Long black hair tied back from his face. Touch of the tar brush I'd say."
"Harry!" Joe exclaimed. "That can only be Harry! He lives over in the first cottage across the road Squire, but he's been away for months, fishing in the North Sea. We'll let you know if he turns up here before you leave."
"Splendid. I'm going up to my room to rest for an hour or two before my carriage arrives. Don't be afraid to disturb me though, if … what's his name? … Harry? … if Harry comes back. I could have been wandering about out there on the moor all night if it weren't for him. I would like to thank him myself."

But Harry did not turn up that afternoon, either at the inn or at his cottage. Bill Trenchard knew nothing of his supposed return to Bolventor.
"I'd know if he'd been in next door," he told Joe and Sam, after hearing the tale of Harry and Squire Ridge. "He'll be down on the farm with your family I shouldn't wonder, Joe."
"Or catching up with the news at Dozmary," Sam said. "Don't worry Joe, he'll be in soon enough to entertain us with his stories."

Squire Ridge's carriage arrived promptly at seven fifteen that evening, just before sunset as his cousin had arranged.
"We haven't seen him as yet sir," Ellie said, when he enquired after Harry, before setting off for the double celebration at old Squire Bray's manor house. "But I'm sure he'll be here in the morning for his breakfast, well before you leave us for the station."

Not long after the Squire's carriage had rumbled away from the inn on the old turnpike road, Joe's brother Will walked into the bar room.
"Harry's not been down to the farmhouse today," he said, when Joe asked if he'd seen him. "Mother would have said something if he had."
"Well he's somewhere around." Bill was pointing with his pipe at the fire, as its flames leapt urgently on the hearth, reaching far up into the chimney.
"Something's wrong," Joe murmured, as Bill stood up to stamp on the small sparks of fire that were smouldering on the rug at his feet. "I'm going outside to take a look around."
Will quickly followed him, stopping only to pick up the oil lamp from the table in front of the window. They had searched around the barns and the stables, and were about to walk across the road to Harry's cottage when they saw what appeared to be Squire Ridge's carriage, returning somewhat hastily to the yard outside the inn.
"I'll not be going anywhere tonight gentlemen," the Squire announced, hurriedly clambering out of the

carriage door. “We’ve had quite a fright, haven’t we my man?”

“It seems that there’s a robber on the road,” his driver said, climbing down from his seat behind the horses. “We were warned … told to turn back.”

“Someone was on the road to warn you?” Joe asked.

“He was standing out in the middle of the road,” the driver said. “I had to stop the carriage or I would have run him over.”

“It was the very same man who led me back to the inn this afternoon. I am sure of it,” the Squire said. “Harry.”

“This makes no sense at all,” Joe said, shaking his head. “Harry left Bolventor almost five months back, and only returned today. What would he know of the Squire’s plans for this evening? Or of any robber waiting out there on the road?”

“Harry would have known, Joe,” Will said. “He was in the bar, on your wedding day back in April, standing by the fireplace and talking to Robert Wilton, when young Squire Bray came to make the arrangements for Squire Ridge’s stay at the inn. I heard it all myself. *‘Family get-together, carriage to and from the manor house in the evening, September 14th and ....’* Well, come inside Squire. Mr Carter will back me up on this.” He turned to the carriage driver. “You must join us. A stiff drink before you go back on the road!”

“Will’s right, Joe,” Sam said as he poured them all a stiff drink. “You had left us to look for Ellie, so you wouldn’t have heard him, but I should think almost everyone in the room heard what young Squire Bray had to say that day.”

"I was sitting right beside him at the counter," Bill Trenchard said, addressing the Squire, and lowering his voice as though the room was still full of people, "when he told Sam here that you would be carrying quite a lot of money on you. *'Doesn't trust banks.'* That's what he said sir."

"Foolish man my cousin." Squire Ridge said, pursing his lips. "Well, no harm done this time gentlemen, thanks to your friend Harry. I shall be gone in the morning, but it seems you have a problem. A highwayman in Bolventor in 1877! You'll have to watch yourselves."

"I should be getting back to the manor. They will all be wondering what has become of us." The carriage driver was looking decidedly anxious.

"Nonsense my man! Have another brandy! Let them wonder for a while longer!" Squire Ridge passed his driver's glass to Sam. "Can we arrange an escort for this man's journey to the manor house tonight? I fear the scoundrel may still be lurking somewhere out there on the road."

"Will and I will ride over to Squire Bray's beside the carriage." Joe said. "We'll take lanterns and a couple of those old shotguns that were stored away years ago out in the stables. No highway robber will challenge a carriage with an armed escort."

"Those old guns will be well seized up," Sam warned him. "You'd do better to take my pistol."

"We'll take it if it gives you some peace of mind," Joe replied. "But I doubt the highwayman's gun will be loaded."

But no guns were needed as Joe and Will escorted the driver with his horses and empty carriage, on the return journey to the manor house. With their duty done they turned to canter back together towards the inn, leaving the driver to explain the absence of his passenger.

"Looking for Harry?" Will asked as Joe swung his lantern continually from side to side. "I was hoping that we might come across him out here on the road. He's acting very strangely, Will."

"You know something about this, Joe? I saw your face earlier, when I said that Harry was with Robert Wilton when young Squire Bray came into the bar on your wedding day."

"Robert is our highwayman Will. The man who has been separating people from their money and their wedding rings over the past three winters. But Harry had reason to suspect him last year and confronted him, stopped him from robbing the Parson on Christmas Eve. I was there. I saw it all. Harry warned him off, found him work down at Dozmary and we thought it was over. We couldn't turn him in to the law, Will. He has a small daughter who depends on him, and the gun he was carrying wasn't loaded. He had no intention of shooting anyone."

"But now you think that he returned to rob the Squire, and that Harry came here today to stop him. Robert hasn't been around this autumn though Joe. He's normally back from their fishing trips well before Harry turns up."

"That's what's worrying me. Robert wouldn't stay away from his daughter without good reason. I'll see the Squire on his way in the morning, and then ride

over to Palmer's Bridge. Speak to Robert's brother. Come to think of it Will, I haven't seen him around for weeks either!"
"At least we know that Harry is alive, thanks to our Squire Ridge."
"And, most likely, Robert as well," Joe said. "Even if they are acting strangely.
Peter Wilton, Robert's brother, had been given employment at the inn on several occasions during the past year. Joe had told Sam at Christmas, that the Wilton family had struggled to make ends meet, ever since their living had been taken away with the closure of the Palmer's Bridge tollgate; and Sam had been only too happy to sort Peter out with a lot of the odd jobs that had needed doing for years.

"Sorry I haven't been up to the inn," Peter said as he opened his door to Joe, on the morning of the 15th September. "I haven't been able to get out of the house. We have all been ill you see, even the children."
"Is Robert here then?" Joe asked him. "Has he been ill?"
"Robert? We haven't seen Robert since early May. I'm worrying about him now. Thinking that something must have happened to keep him away. He dotes on his little daughter, and there's not a day goes by that she doesn't ask for him."

Squire Bray's horse was tethered up in the yard when Joe returned to the inn that morning; and a small carriage, drawn by two horses was waiting outside the door.
"Have you come far?" Joe asked the driver, who was standing alone, close by to the road. "Would you care to come in for a drink, or a bite to eat?"
"We've travelled up from Looe," the driver replied. "I've brought Mrs Gilbert and her son to see the innkeeper's family. And thank you sir, but I've been asked to stay here."
"Mrs Gilbert?" Joe hurried inside. He could hear the Squire in the kitchen, talking no doubt with Eve, and so he turned towards the sound of murmured voices, at the opposite end of the passageway, in the bar room. Ellie, her back towards him, was talking to a young woman; a young woman with long golden hair; perched nervously on the edge of Bill Trenchard's chair; a small boy on her lap.

As he entered the room Ellie turned to him, her face flushed, her eyes red.
"Joe," she said. "This is Mirrie. Mirrie Gilbert from Looe. She has come to tell us that Harry is dead. He drowned, Joe, two days ago."
"No. No, she must be mistaken. You must be mistaken," he said, frowning at Mirrie. "Harry was here last night. He came back in the morning."

But Mirrie shook her head. "He was coming here," she said, "on the 14th. He told me months ago that he had to return to Bolventor on the 14th. Something he had to sort out … unfinished business. But he drowned, on the day before he was due to leave. I found his body myself, washed up on Looe beach that same evening."

"Harry was a seaman." Joe was sounding angry. "How could he drown in the waters off Looe beach?"

"He went fishing off the rocks in the morning, but he didn't return." She turned to Ellie, tears streaming down her face. "He can't be here Ellie," she said. "I searched the beach for him, early in the evening. I found him. Harry drowned."

"We didn't see him for ourselves, did we Joe?" Ellie said. "The man the Squire saw, the man he described to us, it can't have been Harry. We were the ones who were mistaken."

"I must see him." The colour had drained from Joe's face. "Where is he now?"

"His body is at the undertakers." Mirrie spoke softly. "But I want him brought here. This was his home. He must be buried in Bolventor."

"When did he come back from Scotland?" Joe asked her. "This would not have happened if he'd returned to us then. Instead he had to live on the beach in a cave, fishing off the rocks!"

"Harry didn't go fishing this summer, Joe," Mirrie told him. "He has been living with me in Looe."

"But he told us that you were married," Joe said, "and thought your husband lost at sea. That your husband's brother had found him alive, and was bringing him home to you."

"My husband did come home, but sadly he didn't remember having a wife, or a small son. He recognised me only as the mermaid who had saved him from a watery grave. He had no memories of his life before his accident at sea. And he was different, not my John any more. It upset him to see the pain in people's eyes when they realised he didn't know them, people who had loved him, but had lost the man they'd loved. He couldn't be who we wanted him to be, because he couldn't remember who that man was. He grew angry with me, impatient with Johnny. And then someone told him about Harry."

"Told him what about Harry?" Joe asked, feeling angry himself with this woman who was saying that Harry had been drowned. "He befriended you, that's all. You needed a shoulder to cry on and he befriended you. That's what he told me. He said that he loved you, but that you were grieving for your husband!"

"That was all that they told him Joe. That I made a friend of a black man while he'd been away from us. John had been with us for almost four months, when he found out about Harry. Every day had been torture for him. Living with people who expected something from him that he could no longer give them. Knowing about Harry gave him a reason to leave all of us. *'I had not grieved for him for very long,'* he said, *'I had soon found someone else.'* He took his belongings and walked out of our lives."

"When was this, Mirrie?" Ellie asked.

"Last February, early last February," she replied. "Some people blamed me. I lost friends when I finally lost John."

"Not good friends," Ellie said.

"They were John's good friends. I do not blame them." Mirrie looked up at her. "But then in May,

Harry came back. Harry looked after us. I fell in love with him."
"Harry told me that he was going to see Giles Siddall," Joe said. "To make sure that you were happy before he set sail for Scotland."
Mirrie nodded. "Giles told him what had happened to us … to John … and he came looking for us."
"And you were happy?" Ellie asked her. "Harry was happy?"
"We loved each other," Mirrie said. "Nothing else really mattered to us. Just being together and having little Johnny. And now he's been taken from us."
Her eyes filled with tears again and she stood up to stand beside the fire. Flames leapt up to greet her, and climbed higher and higher, reaching far up into the chimney.
"You are carrying Harry's child," Joe said, moving over to stand beside her.
"How do you know that?" she asked him. "It's not been long. The baby's not showing at all."
"It's a long story," he told her. "A story for another day. You are exhausted. You must stay here at the inn tonight. I'll tell your driver to turn back without you."

Joe rode over to Looe the next morning, to weep for his friend; to sit on the beach where they had spent so many happy hours together, and to try to come to terms with what had happened. He could not accept that Harry had been drowned there whilst fishing off the rocks. The sea would not have been rough on that morning, the weather had been fine and Harry knew the dangers; he was a seaman. He had spoken of friends lost at sea; of men and boys swept off the rocks by freak waves, to drown in choppy waters. Mirrie had convinced herself that Harry had somehow slipped, hit his head as he'd fallen into the water, been knocked unconscious so that he could not save himself, and he had agreed with her; said that this was a possibility. But he could not truly accept it himself. He was preparing to leave the beach and make his way into town; to go to the undertakers to see Harry, and to make arrangements for his funeral to be held at Bolventor, when he noticed someone watching him, from the entrance to the cave where Harry had found his diamonds, only twelve months before.

"You here because of Harry?" the man called out as Joe walked towards him.

"He was my friend," Joe replied.

"Mine too," the young man said, grasping Joe's hand and shaking it firmly. I'm Abe. Abe Simpson. We went out on the boats together, three or four years running. I saw you with him once, a couple of years back, right here on the beach."

"We were lifelong friends," Joe said. "Born in the same year at Bolventor. Came up together like brothers."

"He spoke of you often," Abe said. "Joe, Joe Allen. His blood brother."

"How could this have happened, Abe?" Joe asked him. "Here? Somewhere he knew so well?"

"They're saying in town that it will have been a freak wave that pulled him under, dragged him out to sea. That he must have hit his head and could not swim back to shore."

“And is that what you think happened?” Joe sat down on the sand and Abe joined him.
“There are those who didn’t like him being with Mirrie,” he said. “It has crossed my mind that he may have fallen foul of one of them. I have no proof though Joe.”
“What is Mirrie to you Abe? You see she came to us in Bolventor yesterday, brought little Johnny, and she was saying that she lost friends when her husband left her. That some folk blamed her.”
“She lost more friends when she took up with Harry,” Abe said. “I’m her cousin, Joe, and I watched it up close. A lot of folk didn’t like her taking up with Harry so soon after John left. But I didn’t blame her. John wasn’t ever coming back. I saw quite a bit of him after his brother brought him over from the Scillies, and he couldn’t remember any of us. He was looking for a way out, and as soon as he heard that Mirrie had befriended Harry, he had found his way out. He wasn’t ever coming back.”
“Do you know who told John about Harry?” Joe asked him.
“Only that it was one of John’s friends. That was all that Mirrie knew. I reckon whoever it was had an eye on Mirrie himself. I told Harry that once, but he only laughed. He only saw the good in people.”
“That’s true,” Joe said, suddenly thinking of Robert. “You must know Robert Wilton, Abe. Have you seen him around here lately?”
“Robert left for Bolventor the day Harry died. He wouldn’t have known what happened to him. Harry hadn’t seen him all summer. Robert came out with me on the boat up to Scotland, but as soon as we

returned he went out again, fishing off the coast around Plymouth. I remember Harry was angry when he found out. Said he needed to see him."
"But you saw Robert on the thirteenth?"
"I was on the harbour when their boat came in. I told him Harry wanted to speak with him, but he said he was going straight home, to see his little girl. *'No time to waste,'* that's what he said. He was keeping out of Harry's way for some reason. That's what I think. He'll be upset though when he hears what's happened. They were close those two."
"It seems Robert was keeping out of everyone's way this summer, and I think I know why. Do you believe in ghosts, Abe?"
"Ghosts? No. Well I've never seen one. Why?"
"Just a thought that's all," Joe said, scrambling up from the sand. "I must pay a visit to the undertaker while I'm here. Arrange for Harry's body to be taken home. Mirrie wants him buried in Bolventor."
"In Bolventor? But she won't be able to visit his grave if it's in Bolventor."
"Not if she returns to Looe to live. Does Mirrie have close family here Abe? Anyone other than yourself that is?"
"Only my parents and my brother. Mirrie was an only child, and she lost both her parents a few years back, not long before she married John."
"I don't think she should know of our suspicions over the way that Harry died. As you say, we have no proof, and Mirrie has enough grief to bear without thinking that he may have been murdered, simply because he was with her."

"Could I stay here Mrs Carter?" Mirrie asked Eve, early the following morning. "Could I stay at the inn until after the funeral? I have the money to pay you."
"You and little Johnny are welcome to stay for as long as you wish my dear," Eve told her, "and I'll not take a penny from you. We are all grieving for Harry. It's only right that we should grieve together. And there are decisions that are yours to make. We need you here Mirrie, not miles away from us in Looe."
"I am not so sure that Joe wants me here," Mirrie said. "He was very angry when I told him of Harry's death."
"It fell on you to tell him, my dear," Eve said. "That is why it seemed as though he was angry with you. He was angry with Harry for not coming home sooner. Ellie told me that. But Harry was his own man, Mirrie, and Joe will remember that soon enough. He told me himself that Harry couldn't settle anywhere for too long after his grandmother died. But I believe he would have settled down with you, had he lived. Ellie also told me that Joe mellowed a little when he realised that you were carrying Harry's child. And he will accept you for yourself before long Mirrie, believe me. I know Joe. He is a very dear young man."
"How did he know about the baby?" Mirrie asked. "No one else knew except for Harry."
"The inn told him, my dear. It is a very strange story, and a true one, but since it was Joe's story, as well as Harry's, I will leave it for him to tell you."

Mirrie's fears about Joe's feelings towards her were thankfully dispelled in the evening of that very same day.
"Joe is back and he has company," Ellie said, watching from the kitchen window as her husband jumped quickly down from his horse, to help his fellow traveller dismount.
Mirrie joined her at the window. "It's Abe!" she said. "He has brought my cousin Abe with him! Your mother is right, Ellie. Joe is a dear young man."

"He didn't mention that he couldn't ride!" Joe was smiling as the two young women joined them in the yard, and Mirrie threw herself into Abe's open arms. "It's taken us an age to cross the moor!"

"We thought it might help if you had someone of your own around for a day or two," Joe told Mirrie later, as they all sat together in the bar. "We'll go tomorrow to see the parson, make arrangements for the church service and the burial. I'll ride back with Abe when he leaves, see him safely home before I speak with the undertaker again. We were thinking, Mirrie, that you may want your family and friends here with you for the funeral. Speak to Abe about it. He can have a word with them."
"Giles Siddall," Mirrie said. "He will want to come. And my aunt and uncle, and Abe's brother Ben. They all stood by me after John left us. And Harry's friends, men who were with him out on the boats, some of them may wish to come to his funeral."

"Abe will know who his friends were," Joe said, watching Mirrie's cousin as he sat with Ellie up to the bar, little Johnny on his knee. "We plan to ride back together with the coffin Mirrie, escort Harry across the moor."
"As far as I know," she said, smiling when Joe had thought that she might cry, "today was the first day that my cousin has ever attempted to ride a horse. He may need a few lessons while he is here Joe."
"His time here should be spent with you Mirrie, not riding around the roads and tracks on horseback. He borrowed that horse from a farmer friend of your uncle's. The man may not mind if Abe spends a few more hours riding around Looe, though the ride back across the moor should be practice enough. He did well today, for a beginner."
"Shall I take Johnny up to his bed, Mirrie?" Ellie asked as she joined them, carrying the boy in her arms. "He is falling asleep on Abe's lap."
"I'll take him up, Ellie. I always rest beside him for a while, to make sure that he settles. Sometimes I fall asleep myself, and don't wake until morning."
"Before you go upstairs Mirrie," Joe said, "there is something that I must ask you, something that's been puzzling me? Was Harry wearing his pendant when he died? His moonstone pendant?"
"The pendant that had always brought him luck, especially when he went out fishing." Mirrie sighed. "No Joe, he wasn't. He couldn't find it that morning. Johnny had hidden it away. It was a game that they always played together. Hiding the pendant from each other and then seeking it out. Johnny was still fast asleep when Harry was ready to leave the

cottage. He didn't want to wake him, and he didn't have the time to look for it himself. He said that he was late. That he was meeting someone."

"Do you know who he was meeting, Mirrie?" Joe asked her.

"He didn't say, but it would have been one of his friends. I have the pendant with me though. I found it in the chest of drawers beside the bed. Will you take it to the undertaker, Joe? Am I right to think that Harry would have wanted it buried with him?"

Joe nodded. Harry had promised to give the pendant to Ellie one day, when he no longer felt that he needed it himself, but that was before he had found a woman of his own. If it gave Mirrie some peace of mind to place the pendant in the coffin with Harry, then so be it.

"I wore it on my wedding day," Ellie said, taking Mirrie's hand in hers. "And he told me then that it had to be my 'something borrowed'. That he couldn't give it away. It was Harry's pendant, Mirrie. It should go with him."

Every seat in Bolventor's Holy Trinity Church was taken for Harry Reskelly's funeral. A group of his friends had ridden over from Looe, either in horse-drawn carriages; as was the case of Giles Siddall, who had travelled with Mirrie's relations; or on horseback. Local folk came from miles around, to mourn for him and to pay their respects.

As Joe helped his fellow pallbearers to carry Harry's coffin into the flower filled church, he couldn't help but notice Robert and Peter Wilton, standing solemnly together close by to the door. Parson Kellow's funeral services were always lengthy and harrowing. He was known to believe that such services were expected of him, by all those who came to pay their respects to the deceased, and had been heard to say on more than one occasion, that the mourners who attended his funeral services deserved to receive their money's worth, for their contributions to the collection towards the church funds. To this end he stood personally, collection box in hand, while his tearful congregation followed the coffin out through the church door, on its way to the internment in the churchyard.

"Distressing business," Peter Wilton said, grasping Joe's hand as the mourners stood at the graveside after the burial. "I wasn't well acquainted with Harry myself, but Robert was very fond of him. He is beside himself with grief Joe. I haven't seen him this upset since his wife left him."

"I was pleased to see him with you earlier," Joe said, looking around the churchyard. "His daughter will be happy to have her father home again. I would like to have a word with him Peter. Has he left us already?"

"He's standing over by the gate Joe, talking with two of the men who rode over from Looe. He left me and returned to the church, just a few minutes ago. Said he'd dropped his gloves somewhere. But he must have found them because …"

"You must excuse me, Peter." Joe interrupted him. "I have just noticed our Parson returning to the church. I need to speak with him privately." And he hurried away, leaving Robert Wilton's startled

brother to ponder alone on the cause of such urgency.
“Do we have a problem, Parson Kellow?” Joe asked, as he entered the church to find the Parson rummaging through his collection box. “Has someone had their hand in the church funds?”
“So you do know, dear boy,” Parson Kellow said, staring at Joe in astonishment. “It is all falling into place for me now. I saw Robert Wilton coming out of the church a short while ago. I felt uneasy, though I wasn’t sure why. And now this!” He shook the collection box at Joe. “He was our highwayman! He would have robbed me on the night before Christmas, but you knew and you stopped him. Am I right, dear boy?”
“It was Harry who knew, Parson Kellow. Harry who stopped him. I was there but I didn’t know that it was Robert we were waiting for. We decided not to turn him in to the law for the sake of his small daughter. Harry found him work at Dozmary, and we thought it was over. We must confront him now though Parson. He has robbed the church, betrayed Harry’s trust in him. It is unforgiveable!”
“You are too hasty Joe. It seems that our sinner has repented.” Parson Kellow delved deep into his collection box and drew out two gold wedding rings. There are several more in here dear boy, and a silver cigarette case. I will spread the word tomorrow, see that they are returned to their rightful owners. Our brother has returned to the fold Joe, and I am sure that he will not stray again.”

Chapter Nine

Winter 1952

One of the worst winters ever endured by the people of Bodmin Moor brought with it seemingly endless blizzards that made travel impossible; sometimes for days on end. Many hapless travellers, stranded on the road, found themselves abandoning their vehicles and struggling through deep snow drifts in search of the legendary Jamaica Inn, hoping to find warmth and shelter within its old granite walls. Needless to say no one was ever turned away. Derek Reed, a helicopter pilot, based at RAF St Mawgan, further down west on the Cornish coast, was one of these people. He had been sent out on a mercy mission, to drop feed on the moor for the farmers livestock; but his aircraft had been grounded, after losing the top of its rotor blade on Catshole Downs, and Derek, after contacting his base to let them know that he was safe, and that he planned to seek protection at Jamaica Inn, where he was sure that there would be a telephone, was forced to make his way, in the freezing temperatures, across a moor, where in places, the snow lay more than ten feet deep.

It was dark when he finally reached the inn, guided on the last part of his journey by the lights that blazed from her windows, and the smoke that curled skywards from her tall chimneys.

"It's a brave man who ventures out on a night like this." Reg Bray, the Landlord, had come through from the old bar and into the spacious lounge to welcome the man who had staggered through his door. "If you're looking for a bed for the night sir," he said, noticing that his guest was warmly dressed in RAF flying gear, "I'm afraid our rooms are taken, but I can make you comfortable down here in the lounge."

"I'll be grateful for whatever you can offer me," Derek said, sinking into the nearest chair. "I had to bring my helicopter down somewhere on Catshole Downs, damage to the rotor blade. I was dropping feed for the stock out there. Luckily, I'd all but finished the job when it happened, so the animals won't starve. I don't envy them though, out there in this."

"I can bring you a drink and something to eat here," Reg said, after they had introduced themselves, "or you're welcomed to come through into the bar if you fancy a bit of company. Most of our guests have been stranded together at the inn for a few days now. A fresh face will be more than welcome."

Derek followed him through the door to the bar and was soon raising a glass to his new companions.

"I was here a few years back," he said, "when the inn was still a Temperance Hotel. Mind you, we still managed to get a drop of the good stuff from under the counter."
"There's never been a time when folk couldn't buy a drop of alcohol from Jamaica Inn," Reg told him. "Temperance laws or no temperance laws. But now, thank God, it's all legal and above the counter again, so to speak."
"This place could tell a tale or two. I'm looking forward to having a good look around while I'm here." Derek was admiring the pictures on the walls, and the old barrel and lanterns that hung from the beams on the ceiling.
"And I could tell you a tale or two about this place. Stage and mail coaches, smugglers, highwaymen and ghosts, not to mention the comings and goings of two world wars. But not tonight! If you'll help me to bring the settee through from my office, I'll make it up as a bed in the lounge, and I'll stoke up the fire again to keep you warm."

The settee was surprisingly comfortable, and Derek, still exhausted from his trek across the snow covered moor, soon drifted into a deep and much welcomed sleep, undisturbed by the echoes of horses hooves outside in the courtyard, or the noise of muffled footsteps in the passageway that ran along behind the lounge.

He was disturbed though, in the dead of the night, roughly shaken awake, to find himself choking in a smoke filled room. The wooden lintel above the fireplace was ablaze, the flames reaching up towards the beams across the ceiling, and lighting the room. The man who was leaning over him, still shaking him by the shoulders, was urging him to wake the innkeeper. *'Wake everyone,'* he was saying, *'I'll do what I can down here. Go upstairs and wake the innkeeper.'*

Reg, and the other guests, who all came running down to the lounge that night, soon had the fire under control, at first using soda syphons and then water from the kitchen.

"It looks like the fireback has split. Probably frost and snow coming down the chimney. Thank God you were here to alert us," Reg slapped Derek gratefully on the back as the flames were finally extinguished. "We could have all died in our beds."

"Someone woke me. He's the man that we all have to thank. But I don't see him now." Derek said, taking a quick look around the room. "Do you have any other guests?"

"None. And it doesn't make sense. Why would someone wake you and then leave the inn? Let me check outside."

But there were no fresh footprints in the snow outside of any of the entrances to the inn.

"What did this man look like?" Reg asked as he returned to the lounge. "Did he look at all like this?" and he took a picture down from the wall behind Derek and handed it to him.

"Why yes," Derek said, examining the delicate drawing of a young man very closely. "It was

smokey in here of course, but I'd say he looked exactly like this. Long dark hair, drawn back from his face, dark skinned. Who is he? A local man?"
"He was once. But he died, some say that he was murdered, back in the late 1800's. I was told when I came to Bolventor that he's watched over the inn ever since, and now it seems that I've been given the proof.
Take a look at the inscription below the drawing, my friend. 'Harry Reskelly'. It's faint but there's an artist's signature, and a date alongside it.
'Mirrie Gilbert 1878'."

As the lounge was no longer a fit place for Derek to sleep, the settee was returned to its rightful place in the office at the back of the inn, where Derek soon drifted into a strangely peaceful and undisturbed sleep. In the morning however, unable to quite come to terms with the fact that the man who had probably saved his life was a ghost, he returned to the lounge to take a better look at Harry's picture, which Reg had replaced on the wall. As he reached up to take it down again, he was startled by a scuffling noise and turned to see a young man in soot covered overalls, emerging from the fireplace.
"Reckon I can soon put the damage right." The man walked over to shake his hand. "Pleased to meet you sir," he said, eyeing Derek's rather crumpled uniform. "You must be our helicopter pilot. Bit of luck sir, your sleeping down in the lounge last night. I hear you were the hero of the hour."
"Word spreads quickly around here," Derek said laughing. "I gather you're a local man."

"Couldn't have got here otherwise sir. Not in this weather. I was born in Bolventor. Too young to join up in the war, so I've never strayed too far from home. Learnt my trade in the family business." He was smiling, looking down at the picture in Derek's hands. "Our Harry's still watching out for his old lady then," he said. "That's what he used to call the inn sir, *'his old lady'*. It was my grandmother who drew that picture of him, the year after he died."
"So you are Harry's grandson?" Derek asked him.
"No, not me. I'm a Wonnacott, Jeffrey Wonnacott. There are plenty of Reskelly's though, still around up here on the moor. When he died he was living with Mirrie over in Looe, and she was expecting his son. But Harry was a Bolventor boy, and Mirrie wanted him brought home to be buried in the churchyard. She stayed on here after that. She was living in Harry's cottage, just across the road from here, with her eldest son, John Gilbert, when Harry junior was born."
"Reg told me last night that she was married before she met Harry and already had a youngster."
"She was married sir, but her husband had some sort of accident and lost his memory. Walked away from her in the end. That's why she couldn't marry my grandfather, not until years later when she discovered that her husband had died. My grandfather was Luke Wonnacott. He was a farmer's son, but he ran a sort of taxi service out here, ferrying folk around in a covered wagon. That's how he met Mirrie. She asked him if he would take her and her boys over to Looe to visit with her family and then wait to ferry them back again. She wasn't

short of a penny or two my grandmother, or so they used to say. Luke had never taken his wagon as far away as Looe. Liked his little local trips did Luke. To and fro between the churches and farms, local markets, that kind of thing. But nothing was too much trouble for Luke where Mirrie was concerned. He worshipped the ground she walked on. But she wouldn't have him at first. Took him nigh on five years to win her heart, and then my father came along, six years after Harry junior was born. James they called him, James Wonnacott, and she had two more sons and a daughter with my grandfather. Sadly she died before I was born, but my older sister knew her sir. She remembers her well. You'll have to have a word with her before you leave us. She may know a bit more about Harry then I do. If you're interested that is sir."

"Well I'm more than interested. Harry's ghost probably saved my life last night. Point me in the right direction and I'll be happy to visit your sister. Today, if it's not too far away Jeffrey, before someone is sent out here to rescue me."

"Oh, you won't have far to go sir. She lives in Harry's old cottage. First cottage that you come to, just across the road from the inn."

Chapter Ten

Early 1990

The middle field between Jamaica Inn and Hele Farm had been turned into an extensive work site. A new road was to be built across the land that had once belonged to Cornwall's beloved Trelawny family; a road that would run straight through the field and eventually join up with the existing A30, which ran through the centre of the county.

An area had been cleared as a construction camp for the workers. There were eating areas and rest areas; areas where equipment could be stored, and materials stock piled. Heavy machinery had shovelled and scooped, removed the top soil and loaded the dump trucks; torn down the gnarled old oak tree and cleared away all the brushwood; prepared the land for the excavators to move in. Once built the new eight mile stretch of road, starting at Plusha, would form a part of the A30 dual carriageway, bypassing the remaining part of the west bound carriageway at Jamaica Inn; bypassing what had once been the old turnpike road.

As Greg Allen stood on the edge of the old moorland field, an unexpected chill ran down his spine. He looked around him, strangely uncomfortable for the first time in his ten year career.

He loved his work, overseeing road sites and managing environmental risks; working outside in all weathers to improve the road transport system; helping to meet the growing demands of businessmen, travellers and tourists, who were all eager for comfortable smooth journeys and less time spent on the roads.

It had never bothered him before to watch a field torn apart or a tree taken down, but this time he was acutely aware that this land had once been farmed by his own family, the Allen family, who had lived in the old farmhouse across the way for almost two hundred years. He looked around again; the disturbing chill in his spine was more than misplaced sentiment. He was being watched by someone … or something.

He returned to his own vehicle, a works van provided for him by the construction company, to wait for the daily delivery of diesel that was used to fuel the off-road machinery. The delivery truck was running late; probably held up by some traffic disruption. They were working in summer now, in the tourists season. Idly he watched as one of the excavators ploughed its way laboriously across the field, and then came to an abrupt halt, its bucket raised in the air and held aloft as the driver jumped out and ran to the front of his machine. Greg, instantly recognising the man as an experienced driver who had worked with him on other construction projects, speedily left his van to run across the field towards him.

"We've got a body, Mr Allen," the driver said, as Greg appeared beside him. "I was digging out the last of the old tree roots when I spotted it. No more than bones left now though. It's lucky the bucket didn't scrape them up."

"Bones, and some sort of old uniform, Steve. I'm not sure what to make of his clothes."

The skeleton was a gruesome sight, still dressed in the ragged remains of a short dark coat, a neckerchief, a pair of baggy trousers and shoes. What had once been a tight and wide leather belt had helped to hold the coat together. To one side of the body lay a pair of flintlock pistols, and to the other, the crumbled remnants of a high hat.

"An old customs officer, Mr Allen, I'd stake my life on it. There's a print on the wall in my local at Cawsand, of a Cornish revenue man dressed in pretty much the same way."

"Undisturbed for centuries then Steve. Makes you wonder what brought him inland to Bodmin Moor. I'll let the authorities know right away. The men will have to stop work for a while, but keep them away from the body, will you Steve? I reckon this is going to hold us up for days!"

The police arrived within the hour, followed shortly by a doctor from nearby Bodmin. Between them they very soon concluded that the burial was not recent. A local forensic expert from Plymouth was called in that same morning, to determine the age of the remains. He also quite quickly concluded, that while the bones were not brittle, because of the preservative effects of the moorland soil, they had nevertheless been buried beneath that soil for at least two hundred years.

Informed by the police that construction in the immediate area would have to be halted for the time being, in order to call in archaeologists, Greg returned to his works van to contact and consult with the developers.

It was mid-afternoon before he realised that he hadn't eaten since breakfast time. The sandwiches that he had made that morning for his lunch, no longer looked appetising; and so he decided that Jamaica Inn, and a pint of real ale, were beckoning; inviting him to cross what remained of the meadow immediately behind the inn, to hopefully enjoy a more filling meal with his pint.

As he walked away from the middle field, and a strangely quiet construction site, he was faced once more with the malevolent presence of that *'someone or something'* that was watching him and again sending a cold shiver down his spine.

"Not long now, my friend," he said, looking around him at the empty strip of meadow. "Not long before they give you a proper burial alongside the graves of your friends and loved ones. Not long now before you can rest in peace."

With the warmth of the sun once more on his back, Greg crossed the stile in the hedge on the western side of the inn, and strolled around the building, through the car park, to the front entrance.

Half expecting to see a dark and musty little bar room behind the old door, he was surprised to find a spacious lounge, well fitted out with tables and chairs to accommodate its many customers.
"You're busy in here," he said as he ordered his ale from the barmaid. "The weather's too good to be spending the day indoors."
"Oh, they like to linger on for a while after they've had their lunch sir. And there's the added excitement today of course, with your men finding a body down on the site. What's happening down there now, sir?"
Greg sighed. His heavy work clothes had given him away.
"Well, it looks like the body was buried more than two hundred years ago. I've been told that our work will have to stop while they bring in archaeogists."
"What if it turns out to be a burial ground?" she said. "That would really be something!"
"Not for us I'm afraid. Something like that could hold us up for months." He looked at his watch. "I know it's well past lunchtime, my dear, but I was

hoping for a bite to eat. Is there any chance of a hot meal?"
"I'll go and ask Chef for you, sir. I know he's closed the kitchen, but there's no harm in asking, is there?"

"Would you be happy with scampi and chips, sir?" she asked, smiling as she reappeared a few moments later. "Chef says that would be no trouble. As it happens, he's just frying some up for his own lunch."
"Couldn't be better," Greg said, looking around at the fairly crowded room. "Where would you like me to sit?"
"If you'd like to eat your lunch in peace, sir, no questions about bodies and burial grounds from the customers, I'll bring it in to the old bar for you. Through the door at the far end of the room. You shouldn't be disturbed in there."

As she disappeared again, Greg picked up his ale and made his way to the old bar, grateful for the opportunity to be on his own for a while. This small room, with its low beams and copper canopied fireplace, was very like the one that he'd expected to find when he'd arrived at the inn that afternoon. He was tempted at first to sit down in one of the highbacked ancient armchairs that had been placed on either side of the fireplace, but changed his mind and chose instead to sit at a small round table close by to the window.

"This is one of the inn's original rooms, sir," the smiling barmaid said, as she placed more than ample

portions of both scampi and chips on the table for her hungry guest. "It's far too small now of course to accommodate the customers, but it has its uses."
"Then this would have been the bar where my ancestors came for a drink," Greg told her. "My family lived down on the nearest farm behind the inn for roughly two hundred years. From the early seventeen hundreds, right up until well after the first World War. My great-grandfather was born here at the inn, and he didn't leave Bolventor until 1905 when he was in his early fifties. I can remember my grandfather telling us about Hele Farm, and Jamaica Inn. He spent some happy days here as a boy."
"He didn't mention any bodies being buried in that middle field then, sir?"
"I wish he had, my dear. It might well have saved us all a great deal of time and money. I'd like to thank your chef for his trouble today, making me a hot meal so late in the afternoon."
"He's gone for a walk on the moor, sir, but I'll thank him for you when he comes back. He's working again tonight, so he can't go too far away when he's on a split shift."

She left him then to eat his meal in peace, but he soon felt his eyelids closing in that quiet room, where a combination of good food, a glass of real ale, and the heat of the sun through the window were gently lulling him to sleep.

"What became of your family, son? If you don't mind me asking."

'Son? ... Family? ...' Startled by an unfamiliar voice, Greg forced his eyes open to see an elderly man puffing on an old fashioned pipe, and watching him from the nearest armchair beside the fireplace.
"I'm sorry," he said. "I thought I was alone in the room. I didn't see you come in."
"You were dozing, son. I wouldn't have disturbed you, but I heard you telling the young lady about your family. I was wondering what became of them, after they left the inn."
"You wouldn't have known my great-grandfather, sir. He would have left Bolventor before you were born." Greg stood up to cross the room and sit in the other highbacked armchair, away from the heat of the sun. "I'm afraid I don't know what happened to my great-uncles and their families. I am hoping to find out a bit more about them while I'm in the area."
"It's your great-grandfather I'm wondering about," the old man replied. "The son who left here with his wife and youngsters in the very early nineteen hundreds. I've heard stories you see, same as you have, but it's never enough is it lad? You always want to know a bit more about some folk, 'specially when they mean something to you."
"Well I know they did all leave here together. My grandfather was their youngest and only ten years old at the time. His brother and sister were in their early twenties. My great-grandmother, Ellie she was called, had always wanted to move back to Falmouth, back to where she was born. Her mother and step-father had been the innkeepers here for almost thirty years, but her step-father wanted to

retire, to move up to Wales. I was told that he'd had a shady past, left London for Cornwall to escape a jail sentence, and that even in his seventies he was afraid of being recognised. I suppose there was more chance of that happening with the arrival of cars on the roads. More and more people stopping at the inn as time went by. When Ellie's parents left Cornwall, my great-grandad, Joe Allen, moved off the moor with her to live with their family in Falmouth. They opened a second-hand jewellery shop in the High Street and never looked back. They did well for themselves, my great-grandparents. The family still own that shop today, that one, and a half a dozen others down in west Cornwall. My youngest brother Jake is working in the Falmouth branch now. He's always been interested in the trade, but it's not for me. I like the outdoor life. Are you related to us in some way, Mr ….?"

Greg turned in his seat as the door opened.
"Oh, so you're awake, sir. I've brought you a strong cup of coffee. Chef's back if you'd like a word with him. He'll be out in the lounge with me now until he starts work again."
"I'll be there in a minute or two, my dear. We've been talking about the old days, haven't we, Mr …?"
Greg turned to speak to the old man, but there was no-one sitting in the chair beside the fireplace.
"There was an elderly man in here," he said, standing up to look around the room. "Is there another way out of here? Did you see him leave?"
"There is another door behind the bar, sir, but there was no one here with you when I came in a minute

ago, or when I came in earlier to pick up your plate. You were asleep then, and I made sure that no-one came through to disturb you. You must have been dreaming, sir. You enjoy your coffee, and I'll tell Chef you'll be out to thank him as soon as you're ready."

As she left the room, Greg slowly turned back to stare at the empty, old highbacked armchair beside the fire.
'Had he really been dreaming? ... '

Chapter Eleven

Summer 2014

The long hot summer brought visitors from near and far to North Cornwall's 'most haunted' and infamous inn, on Bodmin Moor. Attracted by intriguing tales of smugglers and ghosts, they flocked daily to the desolate moorland location to eat and to drink in the restaurant or bar, and to browse in the shop and the museum.

Heads turned as a sleek black Aston Martin Vanquish purred around the car park behind the smuggler's museum at Jamaica Inn. Eyes watched as it prowled stealthily towards the second, more secluded car park, shunning the company of less elegant little run-arounds, and over-sized coaches. As it finally stopped, settling down to crouch in the most sheltered space available, a few of the more inquisitive visitors to the inn that day, looked on as its occupants emerged. A casually dressed couple, in their early forties, stepped out from the car's dark interior, followed by a young teenaged boy and a small girl. They made their way towards the inn,

locking the doors of the Aston without a backward glance. The small girl skipped along happily between her parents, whilst the boy dragged behind them, hands in pockets, self-conscious and moody, as only young teenaged boys can be. His mother turned to smile at him.
"Your father and I will bring out the ice creams, Josh," she said, "watch Ellie for us for a while will you? She wants to play over there on the grass and make daisy chains."
"Daisy chains! Why can't we come into the shop with you?" he asked, staring moodily after his sister as she ran over towards the grass verge at the edge of the car park, behind the shop.
"Because she can't make a daisy chain and eat ice cream at the same time. Do as I ask please. You can take a look in the shop before we leave."
Josh sat on the edge of one of the old granite troughs outside the entrance to the inn, watching his sister as she picked the little flowers and made slits in their stems with her nails. She was chattering away to herself, as she often did, talking to her imaginary friends again. He had asked his mother to tell Ellie not to bring these imaginary friends along on this holiday. She knew how much it embarrassed him. In return he had promised not to be difficult; not to ruin their time together by picking on Ellie and sulking. His sister was obviously not going to stick to her side of the bargain.

They were travelling up to Yorkshire, to spend ten days in a manor house, in a little village on the edge of the Yorkshire Dales. It was said to be haunted;

with rooms that suddenly turned icy cold; even in the height of summer. The holiday brochure had told of some guests being pushed out of their beds, and of others who had heard footsteps behind the walls of their bedroom, walking along corridors which had long since been blocked off. His family were wealthy; his parents owning a string of jewellery shops throughout Cornwall, and this vacation was to be his treat, a present chosen by him for his fourteenth birthday, which was in five days' time. His mother, fearing that Ellie may be frightened if she knew in advance of the manor house's spooky reputation, had decided that they should say nothing at all about it to his sister, even if one of them did experience something; unless of course it was Ellie herself, in which case they might, as she had said, have some explaining to do. They even had a little bet on between them, as to who would be the first to see a ghost, and each of them had bet on themselves.

"Your father's gone into the inn." His mother had returned with the ice creams. "He was telling me earlier today that his family once owned a farm somewhere close by to Jamaica Inn. Hele Farm he thinks it was called. It was years ago now, but he's wondering if the owners of the inn will know where it is. People don't usually change the name of a farm." She handed him his ice cream. "Take Ellie's over to her will you, Josh? before it melts in my hand. She's in her own little world again I see."
"I thought she promised not to do that," Josh said, nodding his head in the direction of his sister. "She's

been talking to herself ever since she started making that silly daisy chain."
"She's only four years old Josh. She's forgotten that's all. I'll remind her again later."

As Josh reluctantly took the ice cream over to Ellie, his father came out of the inn.
"The owner has only been here for a few weeks Eve," he said, "So he doesn't know much about the area. Strange though, his first name is Allen, spelt the same way as our surname. He told me to talk to the bar manager. His family have lived around here for generations, and he was able to tell me that Hele Farm is less than a mile away as the crow flies, on the other side of the dual carriageway. It seems that you can see it if you stand on that little vantage point where Josh and Ellie are now."

Ellie had apparently discarded the daisy chain, and was now sitting beside her brother to eat her ice cream, on the second of four wide stone steps that led to a small platform, designed especially to give visitors a view across the fields and the dual carriageway, to the craggy tors which dominated the landscape behind the inn.

Wandering over to join their children, Eve and Jake Allen stood at the top of the steps, leaning on the ornate, but solid black safety railings that surrounded the viewing area on three sides.
"Hele farmhouse is the one on the left," Jake said. "It would be an easy walk from here if it weren't for the dual carriageway."

"There are a few other ancient looking farmhouses around, Jake," Eve remarked. "It wouldn't have been quite as lonely out here as you were led to believe."

"The Allen family arrived to live there in the early seventeen hundreds, my love," he said. "In those days there wouldn't have been another living soul for miles around."

"Who lives there now? Did your bar manager know?" Eve asked.

"She didn't say, but my family had all moved away before the Second World War. It could be empty, or the farm could well have been converted into a very desirable little homestead, complete with all mod cons."

"Well we haven't got the time to find out today," Eve said. "We've a long journey ahead of us. Did you finish your daisy chain, Ellie?"

"No," Ellie said. "But the man took it anyway. He left this for me on the grass."

"What man?" her mother asked, as Ellie held out an ancient looking moonstone pendant on a long chain. "Did you see anyone with Ellie, Josh?"

"No one went anywhere near her," Josh said, "and I'm not surprised, talking to herself all the time."

"Well it's beautiful." Eve took the pendant from her daughter. "Do you think someone's recently lost it, Jake?"

"No," he laughed, "Not recently. Not for the last hundred years or so I would say. Look at the state of it Eve!"

"Well we'd better ask before we drive away with it," she said. "Run into the inn with it, Josh. Ask if

anyone has reported it as missing. It may have even been taken from the Smugglers Museum."
"It's mine now," Ellie protested as her mother gave the pendant to Josh. "Harry said he didn't need it anymore. Harry said he'd been waiting for me to come for it."
"Harry?" Eve asked. "Are you sure you didn't see anyone here Josh?"
Josh shook his head. He'd been longing to take a look inside the inn; ask if it was haunted, and this was his chance!
"I'll see if anyone inside knows about it," he said, and he ran off, clutching the pendant tightly in his hand. He walked in through the restaurant, looking for someone to speak to, but the staff were all busy. The large bar room was quieter, but the girl behind the counter was serving a biker, dressed far too warmly in his leathers, for the temperature outside. The room wasn't warm though, and Josh wandered over to the meagre fire that flickered on the hearth. As he drew closer to the fireplace, the thin sticks of wood in the grate began to spit and to crackle, sending up little flames, as if to greet him.

The biker had gone; the girl behind the counter was watching him closely, and so he walked across to her and held out the pendant.
"My little sister found this in the car park," he said.
"We were wondering if you know who it belongs to."
"I've not seen it before," she said, taking it from him. "Pretty though, if it was cleaned up. You take it home, my love, if your sister likes it. Write your

name and email address down here for me though, and I'll let you know if anyone comes in looking for it."

She handed him a notepad and pen and watched as he scribbled down the details.

"Josh Allen," she said, pointing at his name. "Was that your father who came in just a few minutes ago, talking to our manager about Hele Farm?"

Josh nodded.

"Well, well, maybe there is some truth in that old story after all!"

"What's that then?" Josh asked her, suddenly finding himself eager to learn as much as he could about this inn.

"One of our local legends dates back to 1750 Josh, to the year when Jamaica Inn was first built. The story goes that two young men who helped to build her, lived around these parts at Hele Farm. One of them, Jon Allen, was the son of William Allen, the farmer, and the other, his friend Tombar, was an African slave, who had been a stowaway on a ship from Jamaica. Jon Allen would have been one of your ancestors Josh, and it was said that the flames that rose from the fireplaces at Jamaica Inn, always leapt a little higher whenever Jon or his friend Tombar drew near to them. The inn greeted them as a mother greets her sons. And legend has it that she has chosen other sons over the centuries. Men and boys whose very presence has caused flames to leap up into the chimney, and sparks to shower around the hearth. When you approached that fireplace Josh, those little flames leapt higher. They're still dancing away merrily now, in spite of the fact that there's hardly any wood to burn in that hearth today. We only build a token fire in here on warm days. It's not really needed at all, but the visitors like to see a fire burning in the grate."

Josh could scarcely believe his ears. "But how did she recognise me?" he asked, disbelief in his sleepy, grey eyes.
"Well maybe the ghosts have been whispering together Josh," she said, turning away from him to serve a customer. "But I know what I saw, young man!"

His family were waiting for him, perched on the edges of the old granite troughs; looking up as he reached them.
"No one's been in to say they've lost it," he said. "They said for us to take it home. I've given them my email address though, just in case."
"Good thinking son," Jake said, as Ellie snatched the pendant from her brother's hand and placed it around her neck.
"Harry Rascally said I was to wear it on my wedding day."
"Rascally?" Eve said. "Reskelly? I'm sure I've heard your grandfather mention a Reskelly, Jake." But her husband wasn't listening.
"You'll be wearing diamonds on that day Ellie," he said, "not an old moonstone!"
"Something old, remember Jake?" Eve smiled at him. "Something old, something new, something borrowed, something blue. She will need something old!"

He sighed. You couldn't win with women.
"Let's get back to the car," he said. "We're burning up sat here."

Men smiled and women pointed, as a car with the sinister beauty of a big cat moved smoothly towards the exit of Jamaica Inn's large car park. Josh turned in his seat to look at the moonlit scene on the static inn sign. A smuggler, wearing a tri-corn hat, a parrot perched warily on his shoulder, watched as an ancient sailing ship came to grief on the rocks off the Cornish coast. As the car turned and straightened up again, to glide slowly away on the old road, Josh slid deeper into his seat, reaching into his pockets for his iPod and his ear phones. He could still see the inn sign reflected in the rear view mirror, and smiled to himself as it swung on rusty hinges in a sudden breeze. A smuggler, wearing a skull cap, a large barrel perched precariously on his shoulder, watched as the Aston growled, increasing speed as it headed towards the dual carriageway.

"Can we stay here on our way back Dad?" he asked. "I'd like to spend a night in the inn."
"I should think so son," his father replied. "I was thinking much the same myself."
Eve was searching in her handbag for sweets. "That little bet that we had between ourselves boys," she said. "I have to say that I've changed my mind. My money is now firmly on Ellie!"

Song of the Western Men

'Trelawny'

A good sword and a trusty hand!
A merry heart and true!
King James's men shall understand
What Cornish lads can do!
And have they fixed the where and when?
And shall Trelawny die?
Here's twenty thousand Cornish men
Will know the reason why!

And shall Trelawny live?
And shall Trelawny die?
Here's twenty thousand Cornish men
Will know the reason why!

Out spake their Captain brave and bold:
A merry wight was he:
Though London Tower were Michael's hold,
We'll set Trelawny free!
We'll cross the Tamar, land to land:
The Severn is no stay:
With "one and all," and hand in hand;
And who shall bid us nay?

And shall Trelawny live?
And shall Trelawny die?
Here's twenty thousand Cornish men
Will know the reason why!

And when we come to London wall,
A pleasant sight to view,
Come forth! come forth ye cowards all:
Here's men as good as you.
Trelawny he's in keep and hold;
Trelawny he may die:
Here's twenty thousand Cornish bold
Will know the reason why

And shall Trelawny live?
And shall Trelawny die?
Here's twenty thousand Cornish men
Will know that reason why!

From the Vision to the Noose

Jill Batters

An amicable and much respected local merchant is murdered late one night during a suspected highway robbery, on the road between Bodmin and Wadebridge.

A London detective is brought down to the tightly knit Cornish community with instructions to 'Solve the case and ensure that a culprit is found and hanged.'

With one victim, and a story that eventually leads to three women being widowed, eleven children being made fatherless, and several families left devastated, it is small wonder that over one hundred and seventy years later echoes still reverberate around the area.

But why do these feelings still run deep? Maybe because this is not just another murder case, for as this tragedy unfolds, we find, woven within the intrigue, another quite different story.

ISBN: 978-0-9569189-0-1

The Life of Charlotte Dymond

Jill Batters

Secrets, jealousy and a prediction of tragedy send eleven year old Charlotte Dymond from her home near the Cornish coast at Tresparrett Post into service as a maid at Lower Penhale farm, on the edge of Bodmin moor.

She spends many happy years there amongst the close-knit community, but as she grows into a young woman her beauty causes unrest – and she is drawn back towards her past.

Secrets and jealousy once more collide to doubly fulfil the tragic prophesy.

Two young lives are cut short before their time.

ISBN: 978-0-9569189-2-5